American Pro

The overpriced flat white remained untouched, long sinc
young genius sitting nearby. It was 6.30am on a damp, t
the 24-hour Starbucks store was practically deserted sa⎯⎯⎯⎯⎯⎯⎯⎯⎯⎯⎯ ⎯⎯⎯ ⎯⎯ ⎯⎯ ⎯⎯ ⎯⎯⎯⎯⎯⎯
table, bent forward in front of a laptop and staring intensely at the screen with a look of
unbreakable concentration hewn into his face. A legend in the making amongst his peers in
the bleeding edge world of tech, this was Otto Delvecchio, aged just 23 and equipped with a
mathematical brain that was the envy of many a professor. He had achieved so much
already that precisely where he was destined to end up was anybody's guess. But it was
clear that in his case, the sky was the limit.

Good looking yet painfully shy, he had many admirers amongst his following that were
attracted not just by his hazel brown eyes, floppy hair and clean cut boyish features, but also
by his unprecedented mental horsepower. Regarded as the kind of student who required
very little exertion to outshine his professors but chose not to out of good manners, Otto was
coveted by technology leaders all the way across Silicon Valley and indeed further afield.
Despite a steady flow of highly attractive job offers, he had a great sense of loyalty to his
company *Camarillo Tech* and where some individuals were highly motivated by money, he
cared more about the technology itself and strove for perfection at all times.

His reputation preceded him. At the age of just 12, he had built his own social media channel
which he sold to an undisclosed tech giant just 3 years later for a tidy sum. He then went on
to achieve the highest grades achievable at his high school before heading off to Stanford to
obtain a degree in Computer Science.

The world was Otto's oyster, yet he showed no apparent signs of an ego and he was
respected all the more for it. "Something wrong with the coffee, man?" enquired a concerned
voice from somewhere in the haze of his deep consciousness. Otto looked up in a daze,
forgetting temporarily where he was. "What? No, not at all. I was just getting stuck into
something," he replied to the attentive barista. "That's where it starts," came the breezy
reply. "Can I get you a fresh one, DV?" This was a nickname which had stuck since Otto had
begun his career in Silicon Valley. It didn't bother him, in fact possessing some kind of
shortened nickname was *de rigueur* in the modern American tech scene.
"Nah, I'm good thanks man," returned Otto with a considerate smile. The barista left him
alone to return to his ponderings.

In truth, he wasn't actually spending time on work-related projects. At the precise moment,
all he was able to think about was a side project which he had entitled *"Project Ignoto."* The
name alluded to Italian heritage on his paternal Grandfather's side and meant "unknown" in
that language.

The scope of his new project, hugely ambitious in its scale and conception revolved around
the construction of the world's first super-intelligent AI driven machine, which would aim to
remove all of the emotion from the decision making process that inevitably came to the

surface when world leaders are confronted with the necessity to make crucial decisions. By way of example, scenarios which involve the distinction between saving some lives whilst abandoning others, such as hostage situations, the allocation of medical shortages or complex rescue operations. The question which Otto asked himself was - is it possible to build a computer which will take a truly dispassionate approach to arriving at tough decisions by considering all angles, all arguments and all potential outcomes by running each of them through one complex algorithm? If it is actually possible to build such a machine, would the use of it be legal, humane or even ethical?

He recognised his unique position in not only understanding, but being able to utilise the very latest computer programming techniques, that he may be setting in motion the beginnings of a future entirely run and controlled by AI powered robots, where humans appear to remain in charge but in reality are unable to think for themselves. These thoughts, jostling for headspace along with a hundred others, were racing through Otto's head and weighed heavily on him as it began to drizzle outside and the world slowly began to wake up.

Abruptly, he stood up and snapped the laptop shut as if to draw a line under his daydreaming. Offering a cursory wave toward the serving counter, Otto summoned an Uber via his mobile and made a swift exit to get some fresh air. Getting slightly damp in the rain didn't bother him, besides which he had a call later that morning with Singapore to attend.

The streets were rapidly filling up and people were scurrying to reach wherever it was they needed to go. Staring out of the window of the electric Prius en route to his office on Brannan Street, Otto contemplated life. The driver had suddenly entered a conversation with someone on his headset in quickfire Arabic, at least it sounded like Arabic. The dialogue sounded at points more like an argument than a regular exchange of information and Otto passed the time by musing over the peppering of staccato-like exclamations delivered at frequent intervals by the driver. He wondered quietly to himself, that if you could transcribe the machine-gun like delivery of certain words into a work of art, what would it look like? Would the Guggenheim be interested in taking it? How much would an art collector be willing to pay for it and what would you entitle it? *Syrian style Staccato Speech heard in San Fran?*

Temporarily distracted, he hadn't realised that they had already arrived outside the entrance of his sleek, ultra-modern office building. Catching the expectant eyes of his seemingly harangued driver in the rear view mirror, he nodded his thanks and grabbing his rucksack, pushed open the taxi door. "Oh my god, I think that's him!" came an excited female voice from close by. He spun around to face an attractive young blonde lady wearing a lanyard around her neck which seemed to indicate that she was an accredited member of the press. "It's who, exactly?" replied Otto with an aloof half-smile that belied his friendly intentions. Her enthusiasm somewhat dampened, but only slightly, the lady stated as though she were reading a newspaper "Otto Delvecchio! 23 years old. Genius programmer. Coveted by pretty much every unicorn and CTO in Silicon Valley." Cocking her head to one side, she paused coquettishly. "Handsome young man."

In spite of himself, he felt a prick of lust. It had been a long time since he had allowed himself to get involved with a girl, let alone fool around with one. Work was his mistress - he always maintained this motto - and he was dead set on not wasting his prodigious talent for one second. There'd be plenty of time for that later, he reasoned to himself. Despite these pious intentions - he could admit to himself if not those around him - he would have loved, just once, to abandon his self-imposed restrictions and taken up an offer from one of the many girls who threw themselves at him.

"Do I know you?" Otto paused for recollection. "TechCrunch, right?" "Right!" she exclaimed, perking up. Extending her hand to him, she introduced herself as Stella Faber. Despite his handsome looks, he felt suddenly devoid of conversation and to cover his awkwardness, he instinctively thrust his business card into the palm of her hand. Avoiding eye contact, he made his excuses and asked her to call him sometime.

Half-smiling, half-baffled at his manner, Stella nodded in the affirmative and stepped aside. Feeling suddenly flushed by the unexpected ambush, Otto made for the elevator in the hope of evading early morning attention that would only serve to distract him from his preparation. As if mystical forces had just heard his line of thought and decided to play a mean trick on him, he was accosted all of sudden by Jared Fletcher, one of the few people whom Otto had taken an early and permanent dislike to. Jared was a true sycophant and two-faced individual who worked as a senior project manager and was universally regarded as a brown-noser who would unhesitatingly say whatever the person in front of him wanted to hear, only to stir up trouble for that same person behind their back later on, depending on which way the wind was blowing. It was often said that somewhat cynically, that Jared would have made an excellent congressman.

For his part, Otto would happily have tossed a $50 bill to the nearest person with strict instructions to side-track Jared and help him to avoid the necessity of morning pleasantries, but it was too late. "And how are we doing this morning, young sir?" came the unctuous greeting. Dressed in an ill-fitting suit with a ridiculous bow tie and sporting a double chin that spoke to years of over indulgence at the dinner table, Jared made for a cartoonish like figure.

Sighing inwardly, Otto breathed "never better," suppressing a groan as he noted that Jared appeared to be headed for the same floor as him. "A little bird tells me," pursued the rotund project manager, "that a certain young gentleman is being secretly lined up for a keynote speaking engagement at the Seattle Hyper Hackathon in the fall!" He leaned forward expectantly, slavering with self congratulation at possessing this little titbit of news.

"Really?" Otto courteously returned, wishing he could exit the elevator early and trudge up the last few flights of stairs. Anything would be better than being stuck in a confined space with this guy. "Yes sir. You are *quite* the man about town it would seem, or should that be valley?" There was a slimy, presumptuous quality about Jared and the way he spoke. His diction had a sarcastic and insincere tone which immediately got people's backs up.

"You know, Jared…." Otto replied, searching for the right words with some difficulty, "I've been up half the night and…."his voice trailing off with a mixture of boredom and inertia. "Hey! I get it, young stallion," said Jared, lifting a clammy right hand to deliver a condescending pat to Otto's shoulder.

Grimacing from the undesired contact, Otto noticed to his great relief that the elevator had arrived at their floor and with a curt nod in Jared's direction, he exited the elevator swiftly almost colliding with a collection of executives he didn't recognise that were standing directly in front of the doors and made his way to his booth.

Displaying a style which closely resembled some great abandoned factory with tall steel girders and exposed brickwork, yet packed with quirky modern touches such as hammocks, bean bags and pool tables, this was every inch the modern tech space. "Hey, my man DV!" came a greeting that echoed from the other side of the vast, open plan space. Otto peered in the direction of where the voice had come from. The salutation seemed to have come from what was affectionately known as "the nerdery," an area populated exclusively by highly intelligent software engineers and analysts. These individuals lived up to their commonly held stereotypes in every way - geeky, socially awkward, introverted but capable of wreaking havoc if they chose to do so.

If you required the know-how to shut down a city's entire transport system by disabling the underground system, jamming every traffic light and locking every barrier, these were your go-to crew. Willing to pay good money in order to freeze the assets of some rogue oligarch or transfer some bitcoin to Antarctica? They had the playbook for it. What's more - despite their own considerable brainpower, each one of them looked up to Otto and revered him for his technical wizardry and mathematical brain. To them, he was a titan amongst an already talented field although with his characteristic humility, he would have paraphrased Isaac Newton's famous quote *"If I have seen further, it is by standing on the shoulders of giants."*

Wandering over to the nerdery and the assembled brainboxes, he was cognizant of a general crackling in the air, akin to a kind of intellectual pulse, pulsating in the air. "So, what are you guys working on…?" he ventured. "You're gonna love this," came a Southern drawl, carrying inflections of Georgia if not Texas, thought Otto.

The team leader and only member of that eclectic group with sufficient confidence to speak up proactively was Brad Madison, a 30-something native of Austin and self professed original architect of the "dark web." Having successfully captured the attention of Otto, Brad continued. "This here is gonna be a positive Pandora's Box when it hits all the app stores," he claimed with a smirking relish, looking positively like the cat who got the cream. "Oh? How so, amigo?" asked Otto, his natural curiosity peaked. "Well, see this app is gon' do what cops and politicians have been unable to do after years of trying." "Sounds intriguing, but can you be a little more specific?"

Otto studied Brad as he asked the question. Looking at this guy, no-one outside of the office would ever place him in the category of a super-intelligent, PhD level machine learning engineer. He looked frankly like a backwoods hillbilly and despite his remarkable brain, he wore a vague and vacant look which belied his hitherto unseen capabilities. Dressed in a small town USA checked shirt, dirty jeans and sporting a battered pair of Timberland boots on his feet, he didn't look much like a highly prized Silicon Valley programmer earning $250,000 per year.

Pushing these unintentional prejudices to one side, he watched the team leader start to articulate his elevator pitch. "See, er when different folks drink a beer, a whiskey or whatever, they're all affected in different degrees and ways. Some folks can drink 15 beers and believe they're good to go, but other folks cayn't hold more than a coupla beers before it's goodnight, Uncle Sayum!" Brad spoke with a wholesome, unassuming and lilting cadence which brought to mind images of colonial mansions, iced tea on the veranda and Nascar racing, but in reality he was as far removed from that clichéd idea of the Deep South as it was possible to be.

He continued his exposition. "Now what this here project aims to work out using artificial intelligence, is to figure out the unique roadmap for each individual person and how they are affected in real time. It'll plug into existing health data and build up a picture of the long term risks and help that individual work out their limits. This data can be used by their doctor to make medical recommendations on how to get fit, stay fit...y'all name it." The group around them one by one started to drop what they were focusing on and began to listen to what Brad was saying. "Like, right. So you're saying that this app will basically plug into running apps or cycling apps that they might use right now and extract insights from that data?" posed a 25 year old technical architect named Britney Carter.

"Got it in one, Brit." If this thang really works, can y'all imagine how much easier this'll make life for the cops, the courts? I'm gon have attorneys and counsellor queuing up to kiss my Redneck ass!" A triumphant smile was starting to spread across the Texan's face. "Sure, but how are you going to track the user's trigger points? What I mean is, how will you verify the point at which they start getting drunk, when they're majorly drunk and how this may be affected by what they've eaten, if they're generally healthy..." enquired Otto. "It's real simple," replied Brad, glancing around the group and pausing for dramatic effect. "The user is gonna have to complete little tests as they go. "Over a 3 month period, to make sure the results are bonafide, they'll need to go ahead and tap on what meals they've eaten, what they've drunk and as they're knocking back the old booze, they can either select what alcohol they're consuming as they go or pay for it via the payment integrated app - the number of steps they've taken or exercise they've done will be logged automatically."

"Niiiice," grinned Otto. "This shit could actually work, you know!" Winking conspiratorially at him, Brad ventured "did you ever really doubt it? I mean, this is me building it, y'all!"

A general murmur of admiration bubbled up amongst the huddled figures, rather like the sound of a debating chamber digesting the political fallout after a controversial speech has just been delivered. "So, this was your own idea, or?" ventured Otto. "Hell no, replied the Texan. "This is one of the incubator projects. It came from Barker." Charles Barker was the company's Chief Technology Officer, or CTO and was regarded as out of reach and effectively off-limits to most employees within the company. His own personal "ivory tower" was on the 49th floor of the skyscraper in which the organisation was located and few people were ever invited to his palatial office which was said to be wood panelled and contained a well-stocked drinks cabinet, according to the select few who had made it inside. It was regarded as a microcosm of Las Vegas, presumably without the gambling. Barker reported directly to the CEO who had the penthouse office at the top of the building, the 50th floor complete with a spiral staircase up to his own personal helipad.

"What about you, old buddy? Y'all working on anything interesting?" Brad's question took a moment to register with Otto. "Oh, nothing in particular. Just the usual stuff," he replied awaking from his momentary drift. The truth was in fact that DV *was* working on something very interesting and potentially ground-breaking. As transformational as Brad's pet project was, the concept he himself was working on would be a truly significant gamechanger. If, that is he could get it built and off the ground. Right now, he had an 8am video call with Singapore and a fellow nocturnal techie to attend to. Making his excuses, he made a quick exit from the nerdery across the other side of the floor to his own office. He could have used a coffee to invigorate his frazzled brain cells, but that would have to wait. It was time for that call with South East Asia.

Chapter 2

Trang Nguyen was one of his old college friends and a fellow tech enthusiast. Having worked his way up from poor beginnings in Hanoi via a scholarship and sheer hard work, he was now working for a major bank in Singapore and generally living the high life. Work hard, play hard was a motto from which he could not be swayed. Trang gambled most nights at Marina Bay Sands Casino, had concurrent multiple girlfriends and owned a Porsche 911 at just 23 years of age. The envy of many around him, he nonetheless took his work very seriously and never forgot his humble origins, sending money back to his folks in Vietnam every month by way of thanks for the sacrifices his parents made for him.

"DV! You look like shit, man. What's up?" came the cordial greeting delivered from the other side of the world. "Gee, thanks," DV returned with a sheepish grin. "I hope I'm not disturbing anything? It's just that I can't see any pretty girls in the background?" Trang grinned. "Not tonight, dude. Strictly business. In any case, I have a deadline to hit and no amount of blackjack is going to clear the logjam."

Trang spoke in heavily accented American English and had a curious habit of exclaiming loudly in his native tongue at the mention of anything remotely surprising or unexpected. Not possessing much knowledge of the Vietnamese language beyond standard greetings and ordering a beer, Otto was never quite sure exactly what his friend was saying during these occasional outbursts, but it seemed entirely plausible that they were swear words! The two friends spoke of the respective climate in both locations (despite its reputation for fog, San Francisco it turned out, had enjoyed every bit as much sunshine over recent weeks as had Singapore, although the Lion city easily trumped San Francisco in terms of ambient temperature.)

The discussion subsequently turned to recent industry developments and so they compared notes on new innovations and great leaps forward in technological achievement. No irregular catch up between old friends with a great distance between them would be complete without some element of gossip about former colleagues and acquaintances long absent from their everyday lives. They shared a joke or two about Otto's vexatious co-worker, Jared Fletcher who had accosted him in the elevator only an hour before their conversation. "He really is a douchebag," was the American's rather disparaging summary of his Project Manager colleague. "Well, it's true that I have not met this guy, but the way you describe him….let's just say I wouldn't want to get stuck with him in an elevator," offered Trang supportively. The conversation gradually turned to current projects and what problems were keeping them both awake at night. "Look, Trang. This is strictly off the record. No NDA, just the unbreakable trust of friends…." began Otto, confidentially. "You don't even need to say it, man," assured Trang. Otto took a long in-take of breath before imparting his closely guarded secret.

"I'm working on something potentially explosive. Where shall I begin? OK...I'm trying to build an uber-smart machine. Pure-play AI. It'll take computer based intelligence to a whole new level. If I am successful, it will be capable of rapidly calculating decisions based on greater rationality than any human in the history of the world. It will look at every possible scenario and every possible outcome before selecting the right one. That analysis will be completed in seconds and then presented to a select group of advisors, scientists, think tanks….whatever. The capabilities are so far reaching that I can't sleep at night. I'm grappling with the whole thing. I'm 99% sure that I can build it, but I'm also 99% sure that I cannot predict the consequences…."

He paused, having become breathless in his efforts to get all of his ideas across in one go and to summarise as accurately as possible what he had in mind, before his friend had time to interject.

Trang leaned back in his chair, placed his arms behind his head and let out a barely audible whistle. He searched for the right words in which to express his initial reaction. "First of all, DV. Kudos to you, man. This is big sky thinking. Limitless imagination and with a scope beyond anything that is possible now. That's assuming I have understood everything correctly." Waiting for Otto to acknowledge this and receiving a small nod which he took as an invitation to continue, he pursued his thoughts. "We both know how much has been written about AI over the last 10 years. It's the big scary unknown where some over-curious programmer may just open Pandora's Box if they're not careful. Before we know it, we've reached the point of singularity, robots have become smarter than us humans and we're doomed to be exterminated! Right?"

Unsure as to whether Trang was actually expecting an answer in either the affirmative or otherwise, his friend continued. "Wrong! That's a load of bullshit. No lunatic dictator or authoritarian politician is going to allow this to happen…" "They might not get a say in it," interjected Otto. "Hold on a second," said Trang holding up a hand in front of the camera. "I'm not saying that this idea doesn't have great merit; what I am pretty concerned about is that you could build something that would be ripe for misuse in corrupt hands or maybe, that you won't have the chance to get to that stage. Think about it - if you owned the intellectual property to a machine this powerful, consider the capabilities. There'd be a price upon your head, my friend *and* a giant target on your back. You would be walking around with something conceivably more powerful than a limitless supply of gold in your possession. If you want my advice, tread cautiously." Trang then suddenly let out a half-shriek, half exclamation as if to register his absorption of this high level, potentially explosive information with which his friend had just entrusted him.

"So you think it's got legs, then?" enquired Otto, drily with traces of a chuckle at the corners of his mouth. "You want the truth? It's got more than legs, DV. It's got the capabilities to bring down governments and create instability worldwide. Of course, I hadn't considered the possibility that this is what you might be aiming for. "Who knew that YOU would turn out to be a closeted anarchist!" With this, Trang let out peals of good humoured laughter.

Taking up his friend's point, Otto spoke. "Exactly. This machine - if it works - could prove quite easily whether or not governments are needed any more, or at least such large numbers of politicians. If we have a machine that tackles the big questions and makes tough decisions based on rationality, accurate data and assesses all probable outcomes, then why on earth would we need huge parliaments consisting of overpaid bureaucrats in every country on earth, debating for hours on end and agonising over the minutiae of everyday life?" "You ARE an anarchist!" exclaimed Trang with a look of delight on his face. "Seriously though, man. You should get into public speaking. I think you've got a knack for it."

Feeling energised all of a sudden, Otto allowed himself a reflective smile to mirror that of Trang's and made a quiet resolution to himself to continue work unabated on his clandestine project. It must have been how some of the inventors of the past had felt as they got close - often by accident - to the radio, the telephone, the gramophone. Surely, there was an innate sense of curiosity that drove them as well as those other typical human flaws, such as vanity, arrogance, ego and vainglory. He had the capability, he had the modern day tools and know-how. It would have been a terrible waste not to go forward from this point and see where this early stage skeletal sketch could end up. Besides which, he knew that if he was thinking of these capabilities, he was unlikely to be alone in the world so it wasn't unreasonable to assume that he was operating in a quasi-race against an unseen, unknown adversary. There was nothing for it - he had to follow the path and see where it went, despite the urgings of his friends to be cautious.

A sharp rap on the glass door of his small office roused him from his dreams of innovation and breakthrough. A middle-aged Latino lady dressed in a flowery dress popped her head through the door, an air of brisk efficiency about her. "Laurence Siebald on line 4 for you, DV," she announced. Thanking the messenger, Otto told his friend he had to go. "Go get 'em, tiger," came the encouraging response from his friend who, being located 16 time zones ahead, looked like he could use some sleep.

The call on line 4 was from a well known journalist who worked for Crunchbase and who wanted to ask a few questions around a forthcoming product release. Otto went through the motions and answered all of Siebald's questions, somewhat absent-mindedly and then set about performing the many tasks he had in his schedule. It wouldn't be at least until tonight that he would have the chance to resume work on his side project, he mused. Another knock on the door sounded; this time someone brought a warm coffee to him. He was going to need it, that was a given.

Once he had reached the close of the working day, Otto didn't feel like going straight back to his apartment in Nob Hill, so decided to stretch his legs and get some fresh air. Although his home was only 2 miles away from the office, it was just about the right distance to allow for an early evening stroll. Today had been another intense day and as he stepped out into the late April sunshine, the temperature was pleasant enough to make his way toward a bar he knew that specialised in craft beers. His particular favourite was one that was brewed right here in San Francisco, in fact he could almost taste it on his lips. Eager to quench his thirst and lighten his mental burden, Otto arrived just in time to take advantage of the bar's happy hour.

He didn't recognise the tattooed young guy behind the bar wearing a Giants T-Shirt. "Two Hammerheads, please." "You got it," replied the barman casually. No further conversation was offered, which suited Otto just fine and he settled down at the far corner of the bar, out of sight and in a dimly lit spot which suited his requirements just fine. A heated debate was in full swing on a large flatscreen TV up ahead of him. A rolling 24 hour news channel showed a 3-way screen, the anchor positioned in the middle with talking heads either side of her.

The subject of such vigorous discussion appeared to correspond to a tragic accident that had occurred earlier that day in Colorado when a passenger train had derailed in the middle of nowhere, resulting in helicopters flying in a limited number of paramedics trying their best to attend to hundreds of badly injured casualties, very sadly some of them fatally so. Since the accident site was in a mountainous region, there was greatly restricted access for any incoming emergency vehicles, hence the small number of helicopters permissible.
Aside from the usual tit-for-tat blame and criticism game between the Democrat and Republican leaning individuals on the screen, it was clear that the emergency professionals had been doing the best they possibly could given the circumstances and at any events, were faced with some horrible decisions to make. Whether it was a case of serendipity, Otto's thoughts naturally drifted toward his proposed secret machine and what outcomes that machine itself would have predicted in such a real life scenario as this one.

It was a sobering thought for Otto to consider that he, at this very moment, had the capabilities to build a machine for which the drama unfolding on screen right in front of him would be perfectly suited and may yet hold the key to unlock a dispassionate and logical path to the best possible outcome. Outsourcing that great burden of responsibility and its incalculable consequences to a computer, lifting it off the shoulders of an army commander, a head of state or a police chief would fire countless debates about right or wrong, morality and accusations of playing god. An instant message flashed up on his phone. It was from Stella Faber, the foxy press officer that he'd bumped into that morning. Or had she bumped into him? "*I hope you're not working too hard, Mr Delvecchio. How about that coffee sometime?*" He entered the text conversation.

"*How did you get my number? Either way, I'm impressed. As it turns out, I'm in a bar on the corner of 3rd and Brannan.*"

"*I have my sources you know? A girl's gotta do what a girl's gotta do. That's handy, I'm close by on Bryant. Be there in 5. PS let's skip the coffee. I could use a glass of wine.*"

"*If you hurry, you might even make it before happy hour is over (thumbs up.)*

He checked himself, surprised at his flirtatious inclinations. Discipline had been his master as long as he could remember - that's how he had managed to make such strides in both academic and commercial life, he reasoned. Friends and family had often ragged him for his "dull jack" tendencies whilst they were out partying and fooling around. He pondered this and glugged down the remainder of his first beer. It tasted sharp, refreshing and he began to enter that curious headspace that for many exists when the first few beers are sunk and unhindered vistas of creativity and imagination seem to open up and expand all of a sudden. Great ideas come to you as your inhibitions dissolve, yet the basic structure of sense and rationale remains intact, enabling the thinker in turn to articulate and expand on current discussion points. However, quite naturally - in his experience at least - when the 3rd beer was being consumed, the highpoint of inspirational acuity began its inevitable descent.

The entrance doors suddenly opened bringing in a gust of pleasant spring air. She looked stunning. Dressed in a white floral dress that revealed her shapely legs, Stella looked directly at him with a sweet smile, gave a little wave and made her way toward, drawing the admiring glances of most men in the place. There was a real touch of class about her in the way she carried herself - confident without seeming arrogant, worldly-wise without being street-wise, Otto couldn't help but feel mesmerized anew upon seeing her for the second time that day.

He stood up to greet her and managed to knock over his 2nd bottle of beer in the process. Cursing inwardly, he managed to retain a warm and friendly outward expression despite his clumsiness, holding up his hands apologetically and calling to the barman to request a handful of napkins. Stella suppressed a chuckle, covering her mouth playfully which only served to provide Otto with an untimely stirring in his loins. "I was close by anyhow, so I guess if you get us kicked out of here, I know a few other places." Brushing-aside his bungling actions good-naturedly, he gathered himself and having ordered a glass of white wine for his companion and another beer for himself, they sat down at a table in the corner of the room.

Glancing once again at the lanyard around her neck, he made the enquiry "You're a press officer?" She nodded her assent. "That's right. I work for Chuck Rodgers PR agency." "Public relations?" clarified Otto. "Right. Companies who have put their foot in it one way or another will come to Chuck and ask them to come up with a message that deflects the heat off of them, or places the blame somewhere else." "Corporate exoneration services," observed Otto with a sardonic smile. "You get the idea," returned Stella with a winning smile. "I'm willing to bet there'd be no shortage of morally degenerate billionaires across the valley who could use some of Mr Rodgers' advice," suggested Otto. "We're not short of work," agreed Stella nodding her head. "I'll bet," replied Otto thoughtfully.

There was a momentary pause between them as they studied each other's countenance. Stella took up the conversation once again. "So, what about you, Otto? You're the talk of the town. Every time I speak to a CTO or head-hunter, it seems that your name is mentioned yet you choose to stay loyal to *Camarillo* - what's the real scoop? Otto was expecting this line of questioning and had a response pre-prepared. "Well that's just it - I'm not a mercenary. I don't believe in jumping from one tech company to another. It's not my style. If the people around me look after me, then why should I abandon them? Stella interjected: "I never suggested that you were a mercenary, as you put it. But you must experience times where you are tempted, right? Certain people are willing to throw *a lot* of money at you...not only that but think of the perks, fast cars, all expense paid vacations, new emerging tech projects to work on..." "I'm already working at the bleeding edge, believe me," Otto retorted. "Sometimes....it's just a case of *better the devil you know*, right?" Stella didn't look convinced. Maybe, Otto thought to himself, her question about being tempted occasionally was a Freudian reference to giving into his temptation to follow the path *with her*. Perhaps she saw him as a challenge. The quiet, geeky, studious computer engineer who had no natural ability with girls but who was positively there to be seduced. This had to be a possibility, he decided with a flush of excitement.

He resumed his thread. "What you're saying is true, you know. I get approached a minimum of 5 times a day about a new start-up or a new project, yet whilst it's kind of flattering and all, I start to feel a sense of numbness about it all. Does that make sense?" Stella was watching him intently as he spoke. She gave a small nod. "I'm flattered and I'm grateful. I'm working in one of the most exciting industries in the world in probably *the* epicentre of the tech scene. I'm well paid. I can buy pretty much anything I want...." here Otto's voice drifted off. Ever the seasoned PR professional, Stella seized upon the point. "But?" Otto glanced up. Their eyes met. A fire truck noisily clattered past outside, sirens flashing like blue bolts of electricity. The fire truck had disrupted his train of thought. "Shall we head somewhere more quiet?" he proposed.

"I know a great little Japanese place. The sushi is to die for." She looked at him coyly. "You don't mind going for dinner with me, do you?" Trying desperately to hide emerging blushes from turning his cheeks crimson, he blurted out "of course not," in a manner which sounded suspiciously more awkward than confident, stood up and tossed $30 onto the bar, confirming via eye contact with the young bartender that he should keep the change. Helping Stella into her overcoat amid unconcealed looks of envy from every guy at the bar, they headed out into the evening.

Chapter 3

After a 10 minute stroll which consisted of fragmented small talk and the two of them having to politely decline the many leaflets and propositions of assorted evangelicals, human rights campaigners and homeless people, they arrived at the little Japanese restaurant. All of the staff hailed originally from Sapporo and the place had a cosy, authentic feel as a result. They were seated at a table in a dim, candle-lit section right at the rear of the restaurant. It had all the hallmarks of a first date, without the anticipation and build up.

Otto recalled the sage words of a lecturer from his student days who spoke frequently about the need to protect your brains and by extension, your own intellectual property. This wasn't just about patents or copyright, he said. It was avoiding situations where people could coax out of you, through means of charm or connivance, crucial information that could in effect, be stolen. "*Don't walk into a honey trap,*" were his exact words. There was a certain amount of consternation and more than a few dissenting voices toward this use of language, particularly from female computer science students of whom there were admittedly still relatively few at that time, however the white haired old scholar used to justify his argument by the old adage that *sex sells* and no matter whether it's a man or a woman harnessing that powerful concept, the reality remained. To his mind, it just so happened that females were better placed to exercise this ability. Otto recalled the words of his former professor as he looked across the table at Stella. He was unmistakably attracted to her. She was charming, intelligent and very beautiful, but could this be her gameplay, he thought to himself? Almost immediately, he felt a sharp sense of shame for making such a judgement, at least without giving himself the opportunity to get to know her.

"*You're* obviously deep in thought," she said looking inquiringly at him. Her phone started to ring. It was an incoming call from an international number whose country code he didn't recognise. She killed the call and muttered something about this being her down time. Stella placed her phone into Do Not Disturb Mode and suggested that he do the same. After giving it some thought, he couldn't think of any reason to counter her suggestion and followed suit. A courteous and unobtrusive waitress appeared to take their order. "The service here is *super* discreet, you know," she whispered conspiratorially. "Actually, it's my first time here," replied Otto.

The waitress gave him a brief but polite smile as if both to acknowledge this fact and welcome him at the same time. "Would you like me to order for you? I'm kind of a regular." Otto raised no objections and Stella took him by surprise by launching into what sounded like fluent Japanese. The waitress must have already been aware of Stella's linguistic abilities as her face betrayed no element of surprise, but for Otto himself, this was hugely impressive. It was about as much as he could manage to hold a basic conversation in Italian, the native tongue of his ancestors, however he could of course make up for this with his considerable aptitude in various coding languages instead.

Before long, Stella had placed an order for Golden Eye Snapper, Barracuda and Yellowtail Belly to start with Katsuo Don and Chirashi for their main courses. Otto wasn't overly familiar with the cuisine, but his stomach was starting to rumble and he would have been prepared to eat almost anything at that point. Sticking with beer - Asahi in this case - he leaned back in his chair and looked with admiring eyes at the lady opposite him. "So you speak Japanese too?" A flicker of self consciousness passed across her face and she swept her hair back with her right hand. "3 years working in Tokyo." "3 years and you're fluent? exclaimed Otto. "Sorry, but that is almost unheard of." "Well, in my defence, my written Japanese is pretty poor." Otto shook his head in silent wonder. "A lady of many talents," he uttered softly. "It's very nice of you to say," she replied beaming her Hollywood smile at him.

He tried to gauge how old she likely was. Late twenties was his best guess, although it was impossible to tell. She had one of those faces and body types that seemed destined to age gracefully and remain naturally pretty for longer than most. There was a sense of freedom about her that he was slowly starting to find intoxicating. "Let's talk about you," she suddenly announced. He was beginning to feel a little more relaxed in her company and the beer was gradually starting to loosen his tongue. "OK, PR lady," he said half-mockingly. "What d'ya wanna know about plain old DV?" "There's nothing plain about *you*, honey," she shot back in a sultry manner. Summoning up a great deal of willpower to stay focused on the conversation, Otto forced himself to pick up where they had left off.

"Well, here's how I see it. You and I are placed right at the epicentre of the 4th industrial revolution. OK? You had the 1st industrial revolution where water and steam power were used to mechanise production. You had the 2nd industrial revolution which saw electric power being used to create mass production. The 3rd industrial revolution used electronics and information technology to automate production. The way I see it, right now you and I are standing on the brink of a further technological revolution which will fundamentally alter the way we live, work and relate to one another." He paused for breath, warming to his theme.

"What's important to remember is that this has already started. We're actually way down the road in terms of evolution. In simple terms, the innovators and trailblazers have been fusing together technologies which blur the lines between the physical, digital and biological spheres. I mean look at what they've been doing in laboratories, for crying out loud. They sewed an ear onto the back of a mouse. We've built robots that are already more intelligent than humans. We've used NLP technologies to equip backpackers with instant, plug & play translation tools that enable them to communicate effectively with nomads on the steppes of Central Asia despite having zero knowledge of that tribe's language or cultural norms. This is all happening at breakneck speed. Think about it. Those computers back in the 1970s that used to take up entire factory floors had the same processing power as 5% of the smartphone in your pocket. I can't tell you how *pumped* I am to be playing an active part in this space. We should get on our knees and thank god every day, because I don't know about you, but there are no boring days where I come from."

As he spoke, his passion grew and he increasingly became more animated. Stella seemed to be impressed by his zest and zeal. "No, I get it," she nodded in assent.

"There's a lot of unnecessary panic about the singularity theory, but right now what we have to bear in mind is that we as humans are still in control. Scaremongering has a tremendous bandwidth of political currency as we have seen in the recent years and it's often easier for political parties to use mass media, rolling 24 hour news channels and social channels to pump constant bad news out to the world's citizenry. It's the most effective way of keeping people down and controlling them."

"You sound like a true liberal, Otto. Which fits, right? Most key players in the tech industry are democrat-voting liberals who *talk left, live right*," observed Stella. "You mean champagne socialists? Sure, they abound. For me, I abhor politics of all kinds. Politics bore me rigid and I tend to avoid any discussions about right or left. For me, the stuff I'm talking about transcends politics. It's no longer partisan or belonging to one faction or another, regardless of the fact that it can be exploited by either side."

Impressed, Stella tilted her head to one side, twirling her hair in her fingers. "You've certainly got your spiel figured out, Otto and by the way, I don't mean that in a disrespectful way - on the contrary, I find your passion refreshing. There are not many software engineers that I can say that about." The food arrived and they paused whilst the various dishes were conveyed to their table and arrayed expertly in front of them. "It really does look good. It's probably just as well that you ordered, I would not have had a clue where to begin," commented Otto.

Further drinks were ordered and they tucked into the delicious fare, exclaiming at the exquisite presentation and wide palette of taste and colour. "OK, so what have I learned about you so far," considered Stella. "You're a workaholic, you're hot property in the valley but clearly have principles that repeatedly lead you to shun the attention of your corporate suitors. "I wouldn't necessarily use the word *shun,*" grinned Otto mischievously. "Sure. Let's go with *respectfully decline*." "You are definitely in PR!" "That I am," replied Stella with authority. She went on trying to assemble the pieces of jigsaw available to her.

"You have a healthy disdain for politics in general. You have a passion for innovation and someone who believes that you have the power to shape the world in years to come." He scratched his neck bashfully. "I didn't say *that exactly*." She leaned forward. "You didn't have to. I believe I can read people fairly well. I think I'm a good judge of character. It wouldn't be beyond most people in your position to be pretty self-confident if not downright arrogant, but you have something different to offer. A more gentle, compassionate side maybe." She continued to look at him, studying his expression closely. It felt to Otto as if she were looking through him. Sensing a hint of discomfiture, she took a step back and announced that she was heading to the bathroom.

His normal self control and ability to remain centred appeared to be slowly deserting him. Deep down, he knew that he wanted to take this girl home with him and sleep with her, but did he really want to get into a relationship right now. Where did that sit with his deeply held sense of right and wrong and treating people kindly? He saw himself as a modern day gentleman with somewhat traditional views on how to treat women. A sudden urge overtook him and he realised that he needed to answer his own call to nature.

Offering a rather cringeworthy thumbs up to the waitress who was standing nearby, he staggered a tad unsteadily in the direction of the gentlemen's toilets, narrowly avoiding an expensive looking vase on the way. Otto had not been drunk for some time and when a person tends to be as infrequently intoxicated as he was, the effect is often magnified.

Returning to the table a few moments later having splashed his face with cold water, he settled himself back into his chair, exhaled slowly and proclaimed "OK, Stella it's your turn. Let's hear your story." Now it was her turn to try and deflect with typical modesty any anticipation of grandeur. Otto waited patiently for her to begin.

"Well, here goes. I'm 28 years old. I was born into a pretty normal, middle-class American family in Bangor, Maine. My father was a lumberjack, as was my Grandpa before him, my mother was a housewife and I have two siblings who still live back in Maine. Amber, my sister teaches in an elementary school and Jake, my brother works for the Maine Forestry Service as a ranger. We all grew up in a giant natural playground." She looked up at him. "Have you ever been to the state of Maine?" "No, never," he answered. "Well, you really should. It's one of the most rural states of all, huge open spaces and totally packed with grizzly bears. Growing up there was one of the greatest privileges a kid could have had, at least that's how I feel about it." Stella gazed into the middle distance, experiencing a tinge of nostalgia for her youth. "Sounds like we have a tomboy on our hands," teased Otto. "You don't know the half of it, city boy," she returned with a knowing look. He waited for her to resume the tale.

"Bangor is considered a city, but by anyone else's standards, it's barely a mid-sized town. I used to see movies on TV that had been filmed in New York and it all looked like a different world to us. Lumber and Shipbuilding - those were the two big industries in my home town and still are. It's a world away from San Francisco." Twirling her wine glass between her fingers, she continued. "Anyhow, out of the family, I was probably the only one who wanted to break away and experience a different scene, so I worked my ass off, studied hard and ended up being accepted on an international programme that schooled us in the art of public relations. I ended up spending 3 years at the Erasmus University in the Netherlands, then went onto the Hoffmann Agency in Tokyo to work there as part of my final year of study. They made me an offer to stay out there permanently and without any good reason to come back to the States at that point, I took them up on their kind offer."

"How did you find it?" enquired Otto, his attention firmly secured. "At first, I felt like a fish out of water. The Japanese are among the most polite people on earth, for example they are virtually unable to give a straight *no* to a simple request and would rather go around the houses, filling their answer with unnecessary verbiage than directly cause someone to feel disappointment." Otto chuckled to himself and made an observation:- "sounds like a machine learning engineer's nightmare." Stella appeared not to hear the remark. She continued with her account.

"Despite the culture shock, it didn't take me all that long to get used to the place. It's a gigantic city, super high-tech, the transport systems are uber-efficient and they have some truly innovative ways of doing things. Some things seemed completely alien to me at the same time, but I never felt put off or that I couldn't cope... you know?" She looked at Otto for confirmation. He nodded attentively. "The other thing that really struck me from day one is that Japan is a very homogenous society, even to this day. You see very few people of other races and ethnicity, especially outside of the big city. Even though you could say that I grew up in backwoods America, that extreme lack of diversity in Japan was pretty noticeable. But, what fantastic people. I made a lot of friends there and who knows….maybe one day I would take up another gig out there." "Well, it was already on my list but now it's doubly on there!" replied Otto enthusiastically.

Before long, they had managed to empty all of the plates between them and shortly after were presented with the bill which came to just over $100. After some gentle debate in the course of which they both insisted that they would pick up the check, it was decided that the fairest outcome would be to go halves. Those matters taken care of, their waitress went to retrieve their coats from the cloakroom. As they stepped outside, Otto was struck by how far the temperature had dropped. Although they were very nearly into the month of May, it was a cool night and a fresh breeze was dissipating the warm glow of their squiffy state. All too quickly, a cab pulled up right outside the restaurant.

Stella appeared to have ordered the ride via her smartphone whilst she was in the bathroom. Faced with this sudden acceleration in the evening's flow, Otto was caught in a state of flux, gripped by indecision as he considered whether he ought to seize the last ounces of his Dutch courage and make his move, or whether he should revert to type and summon up those deep reserves of self discipline. In the end, whilst he was still evaluating the situation, the decision was made for him.

"Thank you for a lovely night, Otto. Why don't you give me a call in the next few days?" She flashed one of her enchanting smiles at him and raised an arm toward him, offering her hand as she did so. Feeling momentarily like a 19th century duke, he obliged her by taking and kissing the top of her hand which was as soft as silk and smelled of a sweet perfume, the name of which he couldn't identify. "Until next time, Mr Delvecchio," she said, gliding softly into the back of the car in elegant fashion. The electric-powered taxi wafted off into the night in ghostly silence.

Standing on the sidewalk in a mildly dazed manner, he collected himself and pulled out his smartphone to call an Uber of his own. Letting out a groan, he noticed that his battery must have died whilst his phone was in do-not-disturb mode and with no power bank to hand, his decision was made for him. "Looks like I'm walking," he muttered jovially to himself and set out on the 50 minute walk back to his apartment in Nob Hill.

The absence of the daytime office crowd had changed the tone of the neighbourhood significantly and he felt somewhat exposed. Resolving to walk at a quicker pace, his thoughts turned inevitably to Stella Faber. Who was this girl, why had she come into his life and what did she really want from him? Were her intentions authentic and was there something between them? It was hard to be sure. Otto felt drawn to her, there was no point in kidding himself. He wanted to see her again and to spend more time getting to know her. There was certainly a lot to ponder as he strode through the night time streets of San Francisco. Sirens blared and distant shouts echoed as he traversed a succession of neighbourhoods. Luckily for him, he knew the way practically blindfolded, even though it wasn't his normal modus operandi to travel at night on foot.

Otto remained alert and attuned to the potential danger around him and despite the attentions of some loud and aggressive panhandlers as he traversed the crepuscular urban landscape, he arrived home relieved and unscathed just after 11pm. Upon entering his apartment, a long standing habit dictated that he must plug in his smartphone. Having accomplished this task, he strolled through to his bachelor-esque bedroom weary with the exertion of the day and no sooner had his head hit the pillow, he was out for the count. Tomorrow would prove to be a significant day.

Chapter 4

A dream which involved tearing after a runaway train on galloping horseback in an arid wild west landscape merged abruptly into the harsh sounds of an artificial ringtone and the early strands of morning sunshine peering through his window blinds. Otto's alarm clock was programmed to rouse him from his slumber every weekday at 5.30am, but given the late hours he kept, burning the candle at both ends would have to catch up with him eventually. If he were truly honest with himself, he would have acknowledged that he carried a deep seated fear of missing out and perhaps a need to maintain control of his life as a direct side effect of it. His response to such psychological barriers was to simply continue pushing forward, staying busy with multitudes of projects, taxing his brain with ever more challenging conundrums and denying himself the time and space for quiet contemplation.

Yawning loudly, he stretched out - hearing a few clicks in his fingers as he did so - before pulling on his jogging gear along with a pair of Nike Air trainers. This was his normal morning routine, a ritual which he rarely diverged from. Hitting the street before 6am, the city was only starting to show signs of life - the garbage trucks were doing their rounds, exuberant revellers were heading home after a night of clubbing and a million toasters were popping across the state. Aiming for anywhere north of 5km, Otto enjoyed his early morning run. It got his heart pumping and released his endorphins, he felt invigorated and it served as ideal thinking time before the day began in earnest.

His circular route took him past some familiar San Francisco landmarks such as Grace Cathedral and the Cable Car Museum. The steep, sloping streets of the city provided ample strength training for the leg muscles and given the regularity of his dawn forays, he found himself acknowledging many of the same faces again and again as he made his way around the area. Delivery drivers doing their rounds, shopkeepers, kiosk owners and other early risers like himself. Arriving back at his apartment half an hour later, he took a hot shower, fixed himself a simple breakfast and got dressed.

Less than an hour later, he was in a taxi heading to the office when he received a text message from Stella. "How's the head?" she had probed before adding a winking face emoji. "Fresh as a daisy," was his laconic, if not entirely veracious reply. The taxi pulled up at Brannan Street and thanking the driver, Otto jumped out. Half expecting to be accosted once again by Stella - he wasn't of course - he made his way into the office.

As a consequence of his early habits, Otto was generally one of the first employees into the office, which suited him perfectly. He liked to use this time to plan ahead and take care of what couldn't be handled so easily later in the day. This time, he had the elevator all to himself and made his way undisturbed to his office. Seizing this rare opportunity, he determined to return to the idea that was occupying so much of his headspace.

He took a pen and notepad and leaned back in his leather chair. Closing his eyes to aid his concentration, he tried to picture in his mind's eye what a flow chart representation of this "super machine" might look like.

"OK..." he said out loud, to nobody in particular. "It's got to be smart enough to consider multiple arguments, multiple concepts, multiple outcomes and then be capable of evaluating each one of those individually and collectively." He sighed a deep, contemplative sigh. "It'd have to boast the capabilities of learning situational awareness on the go, to understand the predilections of its end users, their own ingrained biases yet contain some kind of artificial logic-based reasoning ability." He rubbed his chin, racking his brain furiously.

Snatching a piece of paper from the notepad, he began scribbling programming code wildly onto the page. It would have taken a highly advanced data scientist to decode what he had written down, let alone determine the direction in which he was trying to go, suffice it to say that the young man was pushing aggressively at the boundaries of what was yet barely possible in practise. If it was possible to see further by standing on the shoulders of giants, then why not use his gifts to help further advance the boundaries and reach of human capability? He continued his intense notation and plunged into a tangled web of fog in which lost all sense of time, a turbulent storm of ideas pouring out one after another in an unbridled torrent of creative artistry.

A giant pulsating flow chart was forming in his mind as he stared down an infinite corridor of possibilities. Connecting the dots in rapid sequence, the outlines of his gargantuan task began to take shape and he became sensible of a metaphorical lightbulb moment as he began to grasp the awesome power of actually realising what had until then simply served as a wildly ambitious concept tucked away in a compartment deep within his psyche.

A sharp rap on the glass door of his office made him jump and he was seized with a flash of rage. "What do you want?!" he almost spat in the direction of the doorway, clenching his fists as he did so. "Woh....jeez! What the heck's gotten into you?" Standing in front of his desk dressed in a Wrangler T-shirt, scruffy jeans and brand new sneakers was Joel Franks, a sales guy in his early 30s with whom Otto had worked on a product launch the previous year. Looking genuinely alarmed at his colleague's unexpected reaction, Otto closed his eyes and raised his hands contritely. "I'm sorry man, I shouldn't have shouted at you like that. I was just up to my eyes in something." He hurriedly swept the pad and diagrams he was working on into the top drawer of his desk and locked the compartment.

Joel's eyes followed his swift action and his face took on a wary look of mistrust. "Something classified?" he asked. The question hung in the air. "Nothing worth mentioning," replied Otto, keeping his cards close to his chest. The awkward silence persisted as Joel's look of mistrust transitioned into one of mild confusion. "*Any-way...,*" he began with the emphasis made to sound as though to his mind, Otto's secretive behaviour was nothing more than a childish game. "These are the draft whitepapers for the new driverless car media CPU.

When you get a minute, can you go ahead and check the technical data for any errors or inaccuracies?" He placed the stack of documents on Otto's desk. "It should be good to go, but the CTO has asked specifically for *you* to check it over." Joel said the word "you" with a subtle yet unmistakable inflection of distaste for the CTO's directive. This wasn't lost on Otto and he cast his own disparaging look on his colleague before running his eye over the whitepapers. "OK. Leave it with me," he told Joel dismissively. With a thin smile and a short incline of the head, Joel left the office silently, leaving Otto to toss the stack of papers aside and with a furrowed brow, return immediately to his previous task.

He sketched out neat rows of equations to reflect as many possible combinations of analysis and calculation as he could muster. Somewhere outside, a cacophony of car horns broke out in a piercing symphony of the urban soundscape. Angry voices yelled at each other distinctly. It was almost 9am and temperatures were rising meteorologically as well as emotionally.

After another 30 minutes of creative outlining, Otto believed that he had the fundamentals in place to start writing actual code. Even though he was a naturally cautious individual and somewhat protective of his work, it was clear to him that he would have to earnestly guard this project. The projected capabilities were far reaching and significant, therefore he didn't wish to relinquish control if he could help it.

An email marked urgent flashed up on his screen. It was from the CTO. "*Got that report, DV? Have it back to me by lunchtime OK>*" conveyed the clear directive. Sighing at this unwanted imposition, Otto shifted his attention to the whitepapers and spent almost an hour going through the verbose technical terminology and identified no fewer than 4 errors. Circling them with a pencil and writing the corrected terms in the page's margin (ironically, his CTO was a traditionalist despite his position.)

His undertaking completed, he headed out to the elevator and exchanged some small talk with a young woman at the reception desk whom he didn't recognise and headed up to the 49th floor. In order to access this prestigious floor, a specially programmed key card was required. Luckily, Otto's ID contained the necessary access and having pressed the button, a soft ping confirmed approval and the elevator soared soundlessly upward.

The external doors slid apart to reveal an opulent, maroon leather set of internal padded doors with gleaming brass handles, designed no doubt to form an imposing centrepiece to the entrance.

Feeling a flicker of nerves in his stomach, Otto pushed the doors open to reveal an antechamber containing an immaculately polished desk at which was seated the CTO's secretary. Her name was Jelinda Chapman and she had worked for Charles Barker as his Executive Assistant in various corporations since the late 90s. He had rewarded her for her loyalty and regarded her as not only his secretary but also his confidante. An African-American woman who hailed originally from the city of Atlanta, it could safely be said that she had the ear of the CTO and consequently there was little that took place in his office that she was unaware of. A larger than life character with sage eyes and a face that was rich in compassion, she was someone whom it paid to be on the right side of if you wanted to progress in the corporation.

Luckily for Otto, she appeared to have a soft spot for him. She smiled as he entered the room. "Howdy, young man," she beamed at him with a Southern lilt. He had a lot of time for Jelinda and felt instantly at ease in her presence. She was one of those unique people who project a sense of calm around them. Perhaps that was another reason for the longevity of her long standing partnership with an extremely demanding, high-powered executive like Barker.

"He's on a call right now, but it shouldn't be much longer." Otto could hear the CTO's booming, dynamic voice through the wall, but it wasn't clear what he was saying. The conversation ended with cordial sounding pleasantries and Otto got the nod to go ahead and head on through.

Although he had been in this room a handful of times before, it never failed to impress him. The sheer scale of grandeur and tasteful furnishings left one with the impression of entering the studio of an interior designer or big name architect. Barker greeted him warmly. "DV! Just the man. Can I fix you up a coffee? Mint tea?" He was a well built, muscular man with a craggy face leaned with creases that spoke of extensive life experience and accumulated battle scars, many of them likely picked up in the boardroom. His piercing blue eyes held a direct gaze and appeared to look *through* the person he was addressing.

Behind him, the imposing outline of the San Francisco skyline seemed to complement the man insofar as it spoke to archetypal values of the American dream - liberty, opportunity and freedom. It was going to be a warm spring day. Sunlight shone through the spotlessly clean windows and created the illusion of a halo above Barker's head.

"Thank you sir, but I'm fine," Otto demurred. The CTO quickly changed tack and brought his hands together in a loud clap as if to underline the new subject. "So, what do you have for me?" Otto reached into his backpack and took out the collection of whitepapers which Joel had been sent to his office with a few hours earlier. "Well sir, I counted 4 anomalies in total which I circled and wrote corrections out for." Handing them to Barker, he unconsciously took a step back as if waiting for a judgement. The CTO scrutinised the papers carefully and didn't speak for at least 60 seconds whilst he pored over them.

When he did finally speak, it was to confirm his satisfaction with the checking work that Otto had done. "Good job, DV." He paused to take a swig of his coffee. The mug had on it a slogan which read *'Me boss. You not'*. How appropriate, thought Otto abstractedly. Barker paused before abruptly changing the direction of the conversation. "Joel tells me you bit his head off earlier. Wanna tell me what's going on?"

This unexpected shift from standing on what he thought was assured ground to having the rug pulled from under him caused him to feel momentary uncertainty. He wanted to remain on good terms with this guy and felt that it was crucial to handle this conversation the right way. Barker had that chameleon-like ability of many senior business professionals to flick the switch in an instant from good cop to bad cop. Those piercing, all-seeing blue eyes of his served both purposes equally well. One moment, you were flavour of the month, next you were being interrogated.

Otto paused and reflected, determined to choose his words carefully. "The truth is sir....I've not been sleeping all that well. How can I put this delicately? I've got woman trouble." Barker watched him intently. He countered, "What's that got to do with Franks? In this scenario, he was just a messenger and we both know that you don't shoot the messenger." Otto continued "I did say sorry to him. I was out of line, I realise that." An incredulous look spread over Barker's face. "Are you kidding me?" he said sharply, his voice rising in volume and his tone suddenly menacing. Unsure how to react, Otto simply stared right back at his CTO. An uncomfortable silence descended between the two men when, just as unexpectedly as his change of tone, a devilish grin began to take over his countenance and it became apparent that he was in fact enjoying a gentle joke at his young employee's expense.

A thundering slap on the back along with an explosive guffaw confirmed the man's mischievous intentions. His disarming smile allowed Otto to relax anew and join in the good natured laughter. "I almost had you there! Ah, that was a good one." Gesturing toward the expensive looking vintage Chesterfield which sat atop a luxurious Turkish rug, he asked the young man to take a seat. "You quite sure you won't have a drink?" "Well, since you've unexpectedly raised my heart rate....I'll take you up on that offer of tea. Camomile if you have it." Barker strolled over to his commodious desk, pressed the button on his intercom and asked Jelinda to fix them up with two camomile teas. Taking a seat opposite Otto, he sat down and smoothed out his chinos.

He immediately picked up on the previous conversational thread. "So, woman trouble, eh? You're a young guy. I'm sure it won't be the first time. Or the last for that matter." He smiled wistfully as though he were thinking back to adventures long buried in the recesses of his memory. "A guy like you will surely have the pick of the bunch? You've got a heckuva lot going for you." Looking expectantly at Otto, he waited for him to divulge some information about the mysterious lady in question. "She works in PR. American. Grew up in the state of Maine. Studied in Europe, learned her trade in Japan." "She sounds like a talented woman," interjected Barker. "She has everything, sir. Brains, beauty, conversation. Grace." This final noun was spoken as an expression of enlightenment, as though it had suddenly occurred to him that this word, more than any other, most accurately summed her up.

"Well, do me a favour. Have fun with her, spend quality time together, let her make you feel good about yourself, but don't let the relationship screw with your head to the point where it affects your daily focus." Otto nodded slowly, contemplative. "Not to sound selfish, but you're one of my A-players and I need every one of you on form and hitting them out of the park day in, day out. There's no room in this business for passengers, DV. That's why we reward you as well as we do. It's a reflection of the belief we have in your, in your value and most importantly, our investment in your development. Damn it, DV. You're one of the most talented young guys in the valley. I'd hate to see you lose your way over some pretty girl.

Right now, you've got a seat on a rocket ship. You're strapped in. You've got some of the brightest brains around you. There's only one direction this rocket ship is travelling in. Don't screw it up! I've seen it happen with other young guys in my time and there is nothing more tragic than wasted talent, I can tell you." He delivered his sermon as a father would exhort his own son to follow his example. The large teak door opened slowly, brushing along the thick carpet softly.

Jelinda entered, carrying an elegant silver tray with practised movements on which stood two fine china tea-cups which held the contents of their recently requested beverages. Thanking his executive assistant, Barker waited until she had departed the room, closing the door softly behind her. "I know you probably aren't going to pay all that much attention to an old guy like me trying to counsel a young guy like you when it comes to relationships, but if you want my advice, play it cool and sure as hell don't rush into any commitments without carefully evaluating the situation. It worked for me." *Not the most romantic approach to dating in the 21st century*, thought Otto privately. He had to admit however, that his CTO had always been good for him and looked out for him in highly competitive situations when he could have played the political game. Instead, invariably he'd had Otto's back and consistently spoken in favour of him despite occasional pressure from his peers to consider trying a different tack.

Sensing that it made little sense to labour the point, Barker changed the subject. They spent a pleasant 10 minutes sipping their camomile tea, discussing how Otto's family was doing, the acrimonious state of baseball, the tech scene in general and what interesting projects were coming out of the nerdery at present. Before he knew it, their time had run out and Barker was due to attend his next meeting. Standing up in unison, they shook hands warmly and Otto left the 49th floor feeling assured and valued as an employee of Camarillo Tech. He knew that the CTO appreciated his work, his sense of duty and his loyalty. If there was ever a time when he encountered real problems, Otto knew that Charles Barker would be his go-to man.

The meeting having come to an end, he went to his office to grab his laptop and headed off to a nearby Starbucks. He had a lot of work to do and did not want to be disturbed.

Chapter 5

Fuelled by strong black coffee, Otto sat alone in a booth in the corner of a Starbucks opposite the Moscone Center working at the speed of light, his mental faculties glowing like an illuminated circuit board. If sparks could have flown out of his laptop, they would have provided an apt visual representation of his intense productivity. He continued onward, constructing complex lines of code one after another, inserting variants and algorithms as he went. Constructing a working prototype was not going to be straightforward, nevertheless he felt driven by an inner urge to realise the scale of his ambitions and it was this vision that sustained him and propelled him forward.

He started to forget about his coffee and a row of half-full cups began to collect in front of his laptop. Given the lofty status he held within his firm, he was given considerable latitude to perform his tasks and that meant a great deal of freedom. Naturally, there were times when he was required to devote practically all of his working day to the development and eventual completion of some new project or concept, but fortunately for Otto, he had just recently seen a major project come to a successful conclusion, hence the CTO's request to proofread whitepapers as well as the Q&A with Laurence Siebald.

A relatively clear schedule was something of a rare luxury for him and he fully intended to maximise it. Realising that he had been holding off a toilet break for too long, he quickly packed his laptop into his rucksack and attended the call of nature. Emerging from the toilets, he noticed with surprise that just over 4 hours had elapsed since he had arrived at the Starbucks. Gratefully discovering that the booth he had just vacated was still available, he returned to the same spot, opened up his laptop and carried on working.

Glancing briefly at his smartphone, he acknowledged a tidal wave of notifications, all vying for his attention like roguish digital gremlins, but he wasn't to be diverted. Resuming his flow of thought, waving away the friendly enquiries of a passing barista, he pursued his quest until the boundaries of a working model were finally constructed. It was late into the afternoon when he'd finally reached the point he was aiming for. This was an impressive achievement and would have likely taken the average software engineer a whole week to accomplish. Affording himself the luxury of leaning back momentarily, he reflected on the progress he had made. His body ached from being crouched over his machine continuously for hours and his brain throbbed from cognitive exertion.

What have I created the framework of here? he wondered to himself. This was in effect, a machine which could conceivably have as great an effect on the course of the 21st century as the invention of the world wide web. It could be viewed as a transformative tool capable of cutting through the collective inconveniences of emotion, bias and vested interests in elucidating a clear path through to the most considered outcome whilst highlighting the decision points required to reach that outcome. *A force for good.*

Long standing territorial disputes and lengthy drawn-out legal disputes of interminable length could be cut dramatically at will. Seemingly unsolvable deadlocks could be broken and problems of gargantuan dimensions could suddenly be solved. The adoption of such a tool might generate major shockwaves and historical constitutions might well have to be re-written. There was of course a dark side to the genie he might be releasing from the bottle, there always was. Namely, that in the wrong hands, his pet project would almost certainly be used for iniquitous purposes by dictators and rogue states.

As someone who measured himself against high moral standards, he shivered at the thought. His thoughts drifted toward the question of how could he take preventative action against such eventualities? How could he safeguard the world against the misuse of something so powerful. He recalled an exposition he had attended in Seattle the previous year which revolved around the singularity theory - the hypothetical point in time at which technological growth becomes uncontrollable and irreversible, resulting in unforeseen changes to human civilization.

Working at the highest level in the very industry which arguably posed the greatest risk of bringing to market such irreversible changes, he felt a kind of social responsibility to guard against or at least limit the damage that such far reaching technology could wreak on humanity. At the same time, he was driven by an innate curiosity of what was possible, to keep pushing the envelope - the reality was that he simply couldn't stop exploring. A famous quote attributed to Francis Bacon came to his mind:- "wonder is the seed of knowledge." Jerked from his brief reverie by a member of the nerdery standing in front of the booth with an urgent look on his face.

"Where the heck have you been, man?" The quintessential geek, Eddie Clayton wore oversized 1980s glasses, a turquoise polo shirt buttoned up to the neck sporting the slogan 'I **see dead servers**' and navy blue slacks which exposed his skinny, malnourished looking frame. Everything about this guy projected a lack of confidence and a sense of deep unease, as though he was always seeking a swift exit from the current conversation. His eyes often darted furtively in different directions, which lent him a somewhat shifty facade. Otto regarded Eddie as a good guy - hard working and certainly diligent, but found his timidity somewhat aggravating. It was if the guy simply needed to get laid and smoke a cigarette, not that this was likely to happen any time soon.

"What's up," said Otto? "There's an all-hands meeting starting in 25 minutes. No-one's been able to get hold of you all day. Your phone just goes straight to voicemail." Eddie spoke with a slight stutter, his speech peppered with anxiety throughout. Both of them glanced at the mobile which was placed face-down on the table. At that precise moment, Otto had no desire to attend the meeting in question; all of his focus was exclusively trained on his ongoing side project. "Can you do me a favour, Eddie?" In spite of himself, Otto feigned feelings of nausea in a bid to elicit sympathy and convey his apologies to those assembled back in the office.

"To tell the truth, I'm really not feeling myself today. I just came here to let the wave of sickness pass, but I think I'm probably gonna head home." He paused to observe Eddie's expression, which to his relief indicated that he had bought his playacting. It was to Otto's advantage that emotional IQ wasn't one of the guy's attributes. It was enough to simply report a condition of ill health to convince him. Under different circumstances, he might have felt a trace of guilt but his determination to throw himself wholeheartedly into Project Ignoto overrode any prospect of feeling such culpability.

Eddie dutifully agreed to convey his apologies and urged his colleague to go home and get some rest. Watching him hurry back in the direction of the office, Otto resolved to somehow make amends for his deception at a later date by owing Eddie a favour to be repaid on some as yet unspecified future occasion.

Not wishing to tempt fate by remaining in his booth and risk accusations of delinquency, he flagged down a passing cab and headed homeward. Ordering a food delivery en route, he prepared for another late night. Traffic was starting to build as time ticked toward rush-hour and office workers neared the end of their traditional working day. His cab driver on this occasion offered no conversation and kept his eyes fixed apathetically on the road ahead. That suited Otto. He was a deep thinking introvert and appreciated every opportunity offered to contemplate the many bulletins circulating in his overcrowded head.

Before long, he reached his apartment building. There was a sweet scent in the air which after some rumination, he traced to a cluster of honeysuckle planted around a trellis near the entrance to his building. Surprised that he had never noticed nor made this pleasant discovery before, he stopped for a moment to enjoy the pungent aroma.

They were almost into May and spring was in full bloom. It struck him that thoughts of Stella had suddenly popped into his head again. The perfume she had been wearing had smelled of jasmine and vanilla, he recalled. Closing his eyes for a moment, he breathed inwardly and drank in the heady fragrance. Resisting the temptation to check his phone for messages - related to both business and pleasure - he made his upstairs and realised just how hungry he was. It occurred to him that with the exception of a rather basic breakfast, he'd eaten nothing all day.

A courier bearing a substantial banquet of mouth-watering Lebanese food saved the day. He wolfed down several Kibbeh to pacify his grumbling stomach before launching into a minced lamb dish, savouring every bite. They had even thrown in some baklava for him. His hunger fully sated, he pushed the dishes away lazily and flopped himself down on the sofa. Sleep overcame him and rather than fight it, he let it wash over him as waves lap over the sand as the tide comes in.

As Otto slept, at a house in Cole Valley, Stella Faber was chatting over a glass of wine with one of her girlfriends. The two women sat at either ends of a sofa, both taking sips of Sauvignon Blanc in between conversation. Stella's friend Jennifer Gresham was an interior designer whose taste was impeccable. Her relatively small apartment was designed with panache and practicality in equal measure, not an inch of space was wasted and she had that rare sense of style which meant in effect that everything that belonged to her was transformed into a perfect distillation of refinement. To the casual observer, her living space was akin to a pastiche of the Art Deco movement, yet unwaveringly modern in its attention to detail. The two women were talking about Stella's dinner date with Otto.

"I don't know whether he was expecting to kiss me goodnight or whatever, but I didn't give him the chance to find out." Jennifer signalled her broad approval. "But you know, I don't think he is the type to take advantage. He's got this sort of innocent, boyish thing going on. Kinda like an old fashioned gentleman in a way," she continued, openly. "Are you getting sweet on this guy?" queried her friend. "I like him," responded Stella rather more quickly than in keeping with the natural flow of their conversation. "Looks like I need to top-up your glass!" Offering little in the way of protestation, Stella gladly allowed her friend to replenish her depleted vessel.

Jennifer looked at her expectantly. "You want the truth? He almost seems too good to be true. He's got the looks, sure. He earns well, check. But it's his brains that are the real turn on! Is that weird?" Her friend shook her head categorically. "No way. If you can find a guy who can tick that many boxes, then you're doing pretty well I would say." Stella considered this and resumed her theme. "I don't want to lead him on or give him the wrong impression, but I do want to see him again. There's something *compelling* about him, enigmatic even. I'm not sure of the exact word. It draws you in. He speaks with such passion. That's the other thing - he'd made one hell of an orator." Jennifer offered her thoughts. "He strikes me as the kind of guy who, once he gets hold of an idea, becomes pretty obsessed with seeing it through to completion."

Stella pounced upon her friend's observation. "Right! That's exactly it. At the restaurant the other night, he was talking about the fact that we're standing on the brink of the 4th industrial revolution and about how far we have come in such a short space of time. We touched upon politics and his healthy disdain for anything of that type. You know, he actually said that what he was talking about actually *transcended* politics. It was intoxicating to listen to. He was pretty much laying out his vision for the future, but that's not all. He totally gets it and understands exactly where we are in relation to the past and what the future could look like. I know it sounds like I'm over-egging the pudding here, but this was literally spellbinding stuff, Jennifer."

"You know what you need to do then," ventured the listening party. "Tell me," Stella said eagerly, with a sudden eagerness in her body language. "Well, it's simple. You need to spend some time with this guy and get to know him. Work your Faber charms on him. You're a pretty special person yourself, don't forget!" Tears came unexpectedly to her eyes and putting down the wine glass, she held her arms to embrace her kind and supportive friend.

Jennifer complied and the two women hugged warmly. Speaking over her friend's shoulder, Stella confided in her friend. "I've always put my career first and dating second. I'm not in the habit of falling for anyone. It's not my style. None of my previous boyfriends were serious - I was always the one that broke it off. I was a little sad yes, but it never felt like the end of the world." Her friend wisely counselled her to keep her head. "Woh, Stella. Who said anything about boyfriend material? You're rushing it a little too much - chill, sister! Besides, how do you know he's not gay?" Stella gave her friend a gentle slap on the wrist as if to admonish such a ridiculous claim. "I don't think so. You didn't see the way he looked at me." Jennifer conceded her ground without argument. "Just kidding. Maybe he is one of those rare breeds that has it all." Stella chewed this over. "Time will tell."

Back across town, the sound of a distant gunshot echoed, causing Otto to sit bolt upright in bed. His bedroom was in pitch black darkness thanks to the heavy duty electric window blinds he'd had installed shortly after moving in and it took him a few moments to equate the receding salvo with his hastily dishevelled composure. Rubbing his eyes sleepily, he exhaled with a deep groan and slumped back onto his mattress. It was that unspecifiable 'dead of the night' zone where inexplicable feelings of restiveness give rise to a general feeling of displacement. It was clear that there was no prospect of getting back to sleep despite his desperate need for its restorative qualities. His thoughts turned to something that Trang had said on their video call. It was something about having a *price on his head* and a *giant target on his back*. A shiver came over him involuntarily as his mind foisted upon him unpleasant images of being followed, tracked, his every move monitored. Pushing those unwelcome spectres from his consciousness, he grabbed his phone and checked his emails.

There was an email from Charles Barker which contained a simple question mark. The subject line read simply "Are you OK?" He closed his eyes and took a moment to stabilize his nebulous train of thought. Hitting the reply button, he composed a brief response to the CTO. *Sick as a dog. Must have eaten something I shouldn't have.* He tossed the phone aside and leaned back on his head, fingers interlaced. Trang's words of warning, although clearly well meant as a note of caution to a good friend, did nothing to appease the twitchy mood he was currently enduring, so he did what he had always done when confronted with an unpleasant sensation in his gut - he went and sat down in front of his laptop to resume the task in hand.

Casting a critical eye over what he had compiled thus far sent a flush of pride through him. Hubris aside, he knew that there weren't many people out there who were at his level when it came to ground-breaking technological innovation. Making an approximate albeit hurried calculation, he estimated that if he carried on pushing forward without interruption, it was feasible that he could have a working model ready to test within 12 hours. It was unlikely to be feature rich and contain the full range of possibilities he had envisaged within the final user interface, but it would be more than able to handle the type of commands he wanted it to.

Switching over to silent mode his general assemblage of various distracting devices, he made himself a fresh pot of coffee and knuckled down with the first peak of his own personal mountain range very much in sight.

Chapter 6

It was another grey and overcast day in Moscow, the biting winter having refused so far to release its begrudging grip. The majority of the giant industrial city's citizenry went about stony-faced and grinding through their daily business with joyless determination. The elusive promise of spring heralded the arrival of green shoots, chirping birds and an explosion of colourful flowers, yet these uplifting elements had failed until now to make a much needed appearance - by consequence, like an obdurate leaden sky, the collective gloom stubbornly refused to lift.

Buried deep underneath Leninsky Prospekt and a veritable stone's throw from Gorky Park, there exists a top-secret and unofficial branch of the Foreign Intelligence Service. Formed in 1991 following the dissolution of the Soviet Union and known by the populace as the "SVR," they serve as Russia's external intelligence agency, holding comprehensive swathes of legally sanctioned powers, whilst keeping such information as their employee headcount and annual budget strictly classified. Reporting to the President with 'daily digests' of intelligence (in a similar vein to that of the American Intelligence Agencies) their role is arguably given more credence on the basis that they actively make recommendations to the President on which foreign policy options are most preferable.

Sat around a boardroom table in a dark, smoky room dominated by wall-to-wall TV screens were 2 special operatives and 1 section leader. The two lesser ranking individuals looked tired and in need of sleep. Their faces were haggard from excessive consumption of coffee and fast food whilst their eyes ached from being trained on screens for hours on end. The chief himself led a small unit of intelligence agents concerned with listening into conversations that could be deemed to fall within the scope of national interest. These exchanges could variously be categorised as potential threats to the Russian nation, useful intelligence in their ongoing battles against designated terrorist groups and information that could prove in the long run to serve the benefit of technological development. What they were doing was of course utterly illegal but to them, the end justifies the means. The mentality equated to "a favourable outcome for Mother Russia excuses any wrongdoings committed to attain that outcome." The section chiefs didn't consider themselves any different or of a lesser moral standing than the FBI, the CIA, Mossad or MI6 for that matter. Whether you were fighting for King and Country, Uncle Sam or Kim Jong-un made not one iota of difference in their mind.

The senior officer looked expectantly at the first operative. Her name was Ekaterina Peskov. Aged 31 years old and endowed with a sharp analytical mind, she was a native of distant St Petersburg and destined therefore to be forever a stranger in Russia's capital city. Plucked from an overseas diplomatic posting 6 years previously to be fast tracked into a career of state sponsored espionage, Ekaterina had long been considered one of the SVR's brightest young prospects. In a male dominated world, she had the guts and the courage to fight against long embedded oppression and felt that she had earned the right to have a voice of her own.

The stern voice addressed her again. "Well? What do we have?" She straightened up in her chair and stood her stack of papers neatly upon the table in a business-like manner. "A great deal of chatter. Most of it banal and inconsequential. It seems that the Americans are more interested in the eating habits of celebrities than the economic prosperity of their country." The chief's face twisted into a sour and scornful look of distaste. A veteran of the Afghan-Soviet guerrilla war, he carried his own battle memento in the form of an ugly, jagged scar on his right cheek.

Maxim Yudashkin was 58 years old, battle hardened and bellicose. Hard-faced and suspicious of everyone, he took nothing at face-value. Regarded as a loyal servant to his nation, he considered himself a true patriot and always took pains to apportion elsewhere any accusations of misdemeanour or wrong doing on the moralistic grounds that he was only focused on doing the right thing for his country. In response to his young colleague's somewhat disparaging commentary on American public life, he returned "It was never different in my lifetime. Capitalism." This last word was almost spat out, with a disdainful venom for whom he perceived as the old enemy. Yudashkin was every inch a member of the old guard and had never forgiven former leader Mikhail Gorbachev for failing - in his unalterable view - to halt the collapse of the Soviet Union.

He turned to the other person in the room. "What about you?" Alexei Zolotov, a 27 year old native of Moscow and renowned hacker put forward his own brief summary. "Much the same, Sir. Lots of conversations about hamburgers...some evangelists wanting to place a large order for ammo on the dark web. They plan to stage a rally on the campus of some University in Tennessee that just announced solidarity with the *Pride* movement. Gruffly, Yudashkin simply shrugged and with an evil smirk on his face, simply said "Good. Let them wipe each other out." Ekaterina spoke up. "There was just one potential conversation of interest which our algorithm picked up." The chief nodded and simply asked her to continue.

"A Zoom call which apparently took place between a couple of computer nerds - one of them in Singapore, the other on the West Coast, more likely Silicon Valley area according to the snapshot. Our NLP tools picked up a few phrases that could be of interest. *Banana Republic, NDA, off-the-record, singularity, think-tank, authoritarian."* These words being spoken in English lent them a curious, metallic sound as though they were unwelcome and unsuited to that room. "It would be most unusual for so many of these to feature collectively in one conversation and so our tools red flagged it as a matter of precaution." Yudashkin and Zolotov took this in. "Any mention of Russia?" enquired the chief. "None whatsoever, Sir." "Then why should we pay any further attention to this conversation?" replied Yudashkin.

"Sir, this is where it gets interesting. It just so happens that the nerd sitting in California is a somebody. He is apparently one of the most sought after engineers in Silicon Valley and is already responsible for a string of ground-breaking advances in computer science." "Does he have a name?" ventured Zolotov. "Otto Delvechhio is his name. According to LinkedIn, he's a real influencer, but is considered more the shy, retiring type." Yudashkin cracked his knuckles and cast his eyes toward the ceiling. He loathed to hear any kind of description that placed a foreign entity in a positive or worthy light.

"So tell me," he said more than a little testily, why should we be interested in what this American kid has to say?" Ekaterina had already anticipated the question. "According to the transcript which we've managed to extract from hacking into Zoom's online repository, Delvechhio was telling his Asian friend about the latest project he's been working on. From the way the conversation reads, it could be something that has a major bearing on the globe as we know it." She'd got both men's attention. Zolotov learned forward in his chair and stroked his chin. "What are the capabilities of this new innovation?" Ekaterina clicked a button on a small remote control which shared her screen to the giant monitor behind Yudashkin. "Take a look for yourselves."

A tense silence descended over the dimly-lit room as if the chamber was holding its breath along with its occupants. The three secret agents slowly took in the translated text and what it all meant. They began to realise that whilst the conversation ostensibly had nothing to do with their nation, nor any other individual nation for that matter, they could easily see the two sides of the same coin. On one hand, this could be a grave threat to their country if it meant being left behind or subject to a game-changing American invention. On the other hand, if there was a way to procure the intellectual property rights to a vaunted forthcoming project such as this one *before* it got to market, there was no telling just how much power that could endow their nation with.

Yudashkin even dreamed to himself that it could mean a return to the good old days. Better yet, what if he could be the one who hand delivered it to the President himself? Salivating at the mere thought of it, he cautioned himself to remain calm and prepare a realistic strategy with which they could progress from here. "If the Americans bring this software to market, they will have the whip hand once again," warned Ekaterina soberly. The enormity of the intel she had excavated from a hacked transcript dawned quickly upon her colleagues. Momentarily, there was a terse silence in the room.

Yudashkin spoke first. "Is the American likely to have a security detail around him?" Ekaterina clacked away at her keyboard in search of the answer. "It's impossible to be sure at this stage. We'd have to put a tail on him and watch his movements for a few days to get an idea of his habits." Zolotov, starting to feel a tinge of jealousy at the way his colleague's obvious triumph was starting to play out, interjected with a question of his own. "What about the guy in Singapore?" Yudashkin looked at him. "Find out. Have a report back to me by 0900 hours tomorrow." Relieved to have made a modicum of a useful contribution, Zolotov gladly confirmed his assent to this command.

Yudashkin perched on the edge of the large table and smoothed out his trousers. He was a tower of a man, broad-shouldered, thick-necked and a face that oozed with grim determination. "We have an asset currently stationed in Los Angeles. Ekaterina, find out where this American lives first. I want to know about his friends, his family, his social life, what his hobbies are, what sports team he follows. A full fact-find. Leave nothing out. We need a full picture if we are to get close to him and discover his weaknesses. I want to know what kind of company he is working for, who he reports to. What makes him tick." Waiting for him to finish delivering his instructions, she confirmed her understanding. "Back to work," he ordered. They complied and hurriedly gathered up their belongings and left the chamber.

Reflecting quietly to himself, Yudashkin went over in his mind what he had heard so far. His young operatives, whilst combing through the detritus of many millions of daily teleconferencing calls that took place worldwide, had observed that one of those transcriptions had been flagged up by automated software tools designed for the purpose of bringing to the attention of his organisation, any which might contain words or phrases considered to be "of interest" to the Russian Federation.

He felt no compunction at what he was doing and would have simply argued in his defence that he was doing nothing different from that of any other international foreign intelligence agency. The question now of course was whether he could obtain the necessary clearance to launch a highly confidential overseas mission. The task was clear from his perspective. To get close to the target, gain his confidence and ultimately acquire from him the intellectual property of his beta version product. From there, it would be ridiculously easy to pass the neatly finished product onto their large software engineering division here in Moscow. They would pick up where the American had left off and guide the programme to completion, gaining all the credit for the homeland, making Yudashkin an instant hero with his President and his people. Naturally, if the charm offensive didn't work, there were always some pretty unpleasant ways of getting what they wanted - and given all that Yudashkin had personally seen and experienced in the field of war, he would have no hesitation to give the order.

His first hurdle was to gain authorization from higher up the chain. There were seven levels of hierarchy between him and the President; in his entire career, he'd never gained permission nor access to speak with anyone higher than 4th removed from the President. It was once explained to him that the reason for this is traceability. It simply wouldn't do for a Head of State to leave behind any trails that could lead back to them, particularly when a difficult or unpopular decision had been made. It was simply expected that others further down the chain of command would do their dirty work for them.

The truth was that he'd been born too late to have been part of the computer age, however he had studied engineering as a young man and was fascinated by how things worked and were put together. This deep-seated intrigue naturally lent him to wonder anew about information technology and its myriad of complexities and capabilities. He couldn't help but feel like a dinosaur in this brave new area at times. After all, in his younger days he had driven tanks in the mountains of Afghanistan and engaged in hand-to-hand combat with the Mujahideen. Nowadays, wars were fought with drones and invisible missiles, not dissimilar to the way people play computer games. Was there a place in this world for people of his ilk any more? He wasn't too sure. He concluded to himself that if he could make a big success out of this large-scale operation, he might call it a day and retire to his dacha outside Moscow.

Ever the soldier, he got to his feet quickly and stood tall in front of the TV monitors with a ramrod back. Bringing his heels quickly together with a click in the now empty room, he began to practise what he would say if granted the opportunity to pitch the mission to his superiors. It was a huge opportunity for Russia, he would tell them. A chance to strike back at the Americans, he would add. The consequences of *not* trying to snatch this potentially explosive machine away from their grasp could leave Russia dangerously exposed!

Naturally, he expected some resistance. The project would be too costly, they would argue. It would be outside of our jurisdiction, they'd opine. For something which isn't definable as a direct threat to the nation, but is in fact pirating by any other name is not something we can sanction. He feared all of these responses. In the end, all he could do would be to state his case as plainly as he could, highlight the likely future threat to national security and do his best to convince them.

He left the conference room and walked through the underground bunker, passing through narrow corridors, crossing room after room packed with busy workers, scurrying around conveying important updates and reports from one place to another. The oppressive closeness of the subterranean maze was starting to make him feel claustrophobic, so he was relieved after a short journey to reach a ladder which led up to a discreet side door through which he could exit to street level. A cold blast of air assaulted him as he stepped out of the building.

The doorway was in a covert location tucked behind a false wall, yet the precise location stood in close proximity to the Lenin monument. You could say that it was hidden in plain sight. Mechanically, he dug a pack of cigarettes out of his jacket pocket, snapped open his old lighter which bore the crest of the KGB and lit one up. The lighter had been presented to him upon the retirement of his former commanding officer and viewing it as a precious item with sentimental value, he took it with him everywhere he went.

Despite the much longed for advent of spring, it must have gotten lost on the way as it still felt bitterly cold out in the open. Taking in a long drag of strong tobacco, he regained his equilibrium once again. Another icy gust howled around him, but he remained impassive. He really was a real life tough guy. Enjoying the calming effect of the nicotine, he readied himself for the upcoming conversation with his superior which could, if he made his case strongly enough, enable the old warrior one final shot at glory. He savoured the thought, images of glory and heroism flashing through his mind. The more he played out these triumphalist fantasies in his head, the more his determination increased. '*I have to take this crown*' he willed himself. '*Failure is not an option.*'

For those who knew what the man was capable of and who had suffered mercilessly by his hand over the years would have rightly trembled at the sight of his remorseless iron will and the sound of his grave words. Yudashkin had been a murderous butcher in times of war, having spared no cruelty where he felt it his duty to inflict it upon the enemy. Behind governmental desks, he was no less ruthless an operator and made a dangerous adversary for even the sharpest rival.

It was time to make the necessary calls. Taking the last draw of his cigarette, he tossed it down onto the hard, frosty floor where it immediately extinguished and, taking a moment to adjust his military cap, he re-entered the building, but not before first checking carefully to ensure that no-one was nearby. Galvanised by his newfound mission, he strode purposefully back down the ladder and through the underground labyrinth staring straight ahead with a look of steel in his eyes. Arriving in his own office, he closed the door and hung his military jacket on the hat stand.

He exhaled loudly and took a seat at his desk. Staring intently at the red telephone placed in front of him, the dead silence in the soundproofed room slowly gave way to the exaggerated loudness of the wall clock, which was robotically ticking away the seconds. Yudashkin cleared his throat in the same way a serpent prepares to strike. He picked up the phone and barked yet another order. "Get me Rosnev."

Chapter 7

It was a true eureka moment for the young genius. Letting out a semi-hysterical whoop, Otto leapt out of his chair and danced euphorically around his living room. He was beyond tired, having worked for almost 11 hours straight on climbing the first peak of his very own Kilimanjaro. The side effects of his long and intense marathon of software engineering read like an insomniac's worst nightmare. The red-raw eyes, blinding headache, rumbling stomach and aching limbs all paled into total insignificance however when he considered what he had just built.

The technical engine which he had single-handedly assembled from scratch was at the very edge of contemporary possibilities in every conceivable way. He had seized upon algorithms and code structures that were simply too difficult or too incomprehensible to the average computer programmer to the point that you would have been forgiven for requiring a theoretical manual with the thickness of a phonebook to have even begun to understand how to make sense of it all.

That was an impressive achievement in itself, but moreover, his system *actually worked.* Whilst it was officially in beta mode and stood in its current form as a mere shell, when compared to what a future completed system could look like, it was perfectly functional. Otto was able to feed multiple strands of intricate information into the platform, draft complex scenarios, multiple considerations and angles of probabilities, yet it still found a route to the most logical, efficient outcome every single time.

The excitement coursed through his veins as a bobsleigh hurtles inexorably around frozen tracks. He'd never doubted himself in his ability to build something as future-altering as this and yet, the fact that he had this living, breathing tool in his hands was scarcely believable, even to him. Like an inventor who has just successfully tested a new contraption which he passionately believes can and will change the course of history, Otto had a deep, inner urge to tell somebody, to shout the news of his achievement from the rooftops. By the same token, he knew instinctively the unforeseen dangers of doing so, therefore he held himself in reserve. The time for a great unveiling would come. At least it might - he hadn't worked it out yet. The possibilities overflowed as a geyser spurts hot steam.

The sound of his apartment buzzer jolted him back to reality. *Who the hell could that be?* he wondered, with a trace of nervous paranoia. Dashing barefoot across to the video door entry system he'd had installed shortly after moving in. Quite apart from filtering out unwanted entreaties, it was a useful device to assess what guests turned up unexpectedly outside his building. To his half surprise, half excitement it was Stella Faber. She looked incredible despite being dressed more casually than in their previous meeting. Dark blue skinny jeans, a black turtle neck jumper and a cherry red cropped leather jacket formed her stylish look, topped off with a rather expensive looking pair of black shoes.

"Pleased to see me?" she opened, with that kittenish way of hers that Otto found so irresistible. "A feast for my eyes," he replied meekly, aware of his deficiencies in the sweet talk department. Gesturing to come inside, he was taken aback when she threw herself into his arms. Their embrace was warm and comforting, her sweet perfume infiltrating his nostrils in a kind of olfactory hypnosis. His tiredness mingled imperceptibly with giddiness and a warm feeling of acceptance washed over him. "Come on in. I've got something pretty cool to show you." Slipping her shoes off neatly by the door, she glided across his hallway soundlessly in great anticipation of what Otto had in store for her. He seemed almost electrically charged and had a messianic zeal in his eyes which suggested to her that he was working on something original.

They reached the living room where Otto's laptop sat on the coffee table. Patting the sofa, he invited her to sit down next to him. "I don't know how to say this, but I think I might actually have done it." She looked at him quizzically. "Done what exactly?" He took a moment to compose himself. "You remember the concept I was talking about at dinner the other night? Building a supercomputer that could replace the thought process of juries, political leadership and boardrooms combined?"

A look of disbelief spread slowly across Stella's face. Her expression precluded any requirement to ask the obvious question. "Yup, he nodded. It's looking that way." Stella's instincts never normally failed her and she had a gut feeling that this might well be one of those 'I was there' moments. "Let me show you. One well known scenario that I fed into the machine was a real life example that took place in the summer of 1940. Winston Churchill, the British Prime Minister was facing a terrible dilemma.

France had just surrendered and only the English Channel stood between the Nazis and Britain. Germany was poised to seize the entire French fleet, one of the biggest in the world. With these ships in his hands, Hitler's threat to invade Britain could become a reality. Churchill had to make a choice. He could either trust the promises of the new French government that they would never hand over their ships to Hitler. Or he could make sure that the ships never joined the German navy by destroying them himself."

Stella listened attentively to the story, rapt. "In the end, Churchill did take the heart-wrenching decision to attack his former French allies; I'm pretty sure that it was not one that he took lightly and he must have wrestled with it terribly. He may well have come to the view that when a country loses its will to fight, there's not much you can do to inspire them to anything but quit. Whilst the French army was shattered, their navy was still remarkably intact." Otto paused to take a sip of water and glancing at the notes he had scribbled on a pad, resumed his recounting of the story.

"On June 17th, France pressed for peace with Germany. Before France could officially surrender, Churchill tried to convince his War Cabinet to attack the French Fleet. The War Cabinet refused. There were several concerns on the table. For one, the attack would surely result in the loss of British troops and ships. Second, although getting beaten by Germany and showing eagerness to throw in the towel, France was still an ally." Stella was deeply impressed with Otto's level of research and even more so by his emerging stock as potential boyfriend material.

"On June 24, France and Germany signed an armistice. Part of that agreement was that the French could keep their ships, but Germany would gain control over items such as passports and tickets. Hitler treaded lightly concerning the ships and did not push for full ownership. He feared such aggression would inspire the French to keep fighting. Hitler's concerns were not known to Britain. However, on July 1, Churchill was finally able to get the backing of the War Cabinet to sink the ships if they would not be surrendered.

On July 3, the British surrounded the French Fleet at the port of Mers-el-Kebir right outside Oran, Algeria. Churchill's message was clear: sail to Britain, sail to the USA, or scuttle your ships in the next six hours. At first, the French refused to speak to negotiators. Two hours later, the French showed the British an order they had received from Admiral Darlan instructing them to sail the ships to the USA if the Germans broke the armistice and demanded the ships. Meanwhile, the British intercepted a message from the Vichy Government ordering French reinforcements to move urgently to Oran.

Churchill was done playing games and ordered the attack to his commanders: 'Settle everything before dark or you will have reinforcements to deal with.' An hour and a half later, the British Fleet attacked. In less than ten minutes, 1,297 French soldiers were dead, and 3 capital ships along with 1 destroyer were damaged or destroyed." Stella let out a long, regretful whistle through pursed lips. "While the French were furious over the events, the reaction in the UK was the exact opposite. The day after attacking the French, Churchill went to the House of Commons to explain why he ordered the attack on the former ally.

He declared, 'However painful, the action we have already taken should be, in itself, sufficient to dispose once and for all of the lies and Fifth Column activities that we have the slightest intention of entering into negotiations. We shall prosecute the war with the utmost vigour by all the means that are open to us.' For the first time since taking over as Prime Minister, Churchill received a unanimous standing ovation. Churchill had a message for the British, for Hitler, and for the world. The message was heard loud and clear. The UK would not make peace with Hitler and they were in this war for the long haul."

"It sounds like a perfect scenario for the machine you are building," observed Stella astutely. "Just so," concurred Otto. "Churchill was faced with a near impossible situation. "Although there was political capital available in the sense of brandishing an iron fist in the direction of

Hitler and thereby winning a great deal of support from his countrymen, he had the moral dilemma to navigate and the fact that had the French not been able to scuttle their own navy, the Nazis would have been perfectly placed to launch a long threatened invasion. From that point, Britain would probably have been unable to fend off the enemy, particularly given that we Americans were at that point, resisting their frequent entreaties to join the war effort.

The future of the world would have likely looked very different within the succeeding years." Allowing all of this to sink in, Stella enquired "so what did your machine say about this? What decision did it arrive at?" Otto looked at her in a matter-of-fact way and simply replied "almost exactly as Churchill carried it out." A thoughtful silence followed. "How long did the computer take to appraise all the possible angles and outcomes? Otto replied instantly. "35 seconds."

A deep intake of breath. "Oh my god." "I know, agreed Otto. I was just feeding through another real world scenario through the machine when you rang the doorbell. This one was arguably the most far reaching of all." Stella looked at him with a curious expression. He nodded pensively. "Another World War 2 example, I'm afraid. The dropping of the atomic bombs on Hiroshima and Nagasaki right at the end of the war."

A cold shiver swept over her and she felt a sudden, inexplicable mixture of fear and excitement. Her system spelt out apprehension of the enormous unpredictability to which she was now a party and yet there was an elusive thrill at the way Otto was pushing the boundaries of what was currently possible in predictive analytics and the study of human behaviour. It was like being back in school, goofing around with Ouija boards, playing fast and loose with the mysterious powers of the occult and generally venturing into territories which felt both unsafe and unknown.

Otto suddenly let out a loud and uncontrollable yawn. He looked utterly shattered. Putting a gentle arm around him, she drew his weary head onto her shoulder and stroked his hair softly. Within a matter of minutes, he was fast asleep and snoring softly. Recalling the conversation with her friend Jennifer barely two hours prior, she realised with butterflies in her stomach that here she was, sitting on the sofa with the object of her affection, caressing his head and being in his confidence at the moment of what seemed to be a major breakthrough, even for him.

His intellect was truly intoxicating. The fact that he was young, successful and good looking was merely a bonus. Not merely content to speak knowledgeably about technology, he seemed to know his history too. For her, that was a big turn on. She admired a man who could construct logical and convincing arguments based not only on what could be accurately predicted, but what had gone before. Ruminating at length over what Otto had set out, she observed her curiosity as it began to grow inordinately and, like the apocryphal cat, she yearned to learn more.

A matter of moments later, she was unable to contain herself any longer. Manoeuvring Otto gently so that he leant on his other side, Stella leant forward and took control of the mouse. Much of the interface made little sense to her, jumbled maze of impenetrable code and formulas as it was, however the search bar in which you could ask or type a question of your own making was apparently accessible, so she started to pose a series of questions devised of her own hurried invention, later adding complications and double propositions in an effort to test the resilience and capabilities of the machine. The answers it threw back at her by turns shocked her, stunned her and impressed her, yet in every single case when she took a moment to consider the detailed summary of how the machine arrived at its decision, there was a striking scientific beauty, gleaming with lucidity in its coherence, systematic in its reasoning.

Conscious that she was being drawn in and becoming fully immersed in this captivating, oracle-like machine, she forced herself to take a step back and digest what she had witnessed. If this tool really was able to cut through the noise as Otto said - and from what she had seen for herself, it really did get straight to the most logical conclusion whatever you threw at it - then this was potential dynamite.

She knew instinctively from her years in PR and dealing with some tough and often unsavoury businesspeople that being the creator of an all-powerful tool like this one carried a great deal of risk. Her growing fondness for Otto instilled in her a concern for his safety upon launching a path such as the one apparently opening up before him. He was no fool and he didn't strike her as naive, but some nagging doubt at the back of her mind persisted. Was he tough enough to equip himself against the type of people who would likely come knocking at his door? That she did not know.

Casting a glance over her shoulder at the sleepy figure snoring quietly on the sofa, she thought to herself how peaceful he looked. She looked around in search of a blanket, taking care not to make any more noise than necessary and located one in a bedroom drawer. Placing it tenderly over him, she helped herself to a glass of water and went to lie down on his bed. She assumed that he wouldn't mind overly.

It took her some time to finally drop off to sleep given the sheer volume of items she sought to process mentally. It felt clear to her that she was about to embark on an exciting journey or at the very least, she was due to play her part in a forthcoming drama of some description. Consulting the retro alarm clock on Otto's bedside table, she noted the time: 23.15. Time to at least try and rest, she concluded. By degrees, little by little she dropped into a fitful sleep and dreamt intermittently about computer hackers, unscrupulous businessmen and invading armies.

Morning arrived early, accompanied by beaming rays of sun streaming in through Otto's bedroom window. The relic timepiece showed 6.05 as the time. Feeling somewhat tired, Stella raised herself up with a reluctant effort and noticed with some surprise that the object of her fancy remained fast asleep on the sofa. Without either a change of clothes nor any make up, she was at a loose end but felt as though it wouldn't have been appropriate to have left without saying goodbye.

After allowing herself a moment to come round, she strolled into the kitchen with the intention of fixing Otto a makeshift breakfast. Taking a cursory glance through the fridge and cupboards, she discovered eggs, bacon and English muffins and decided to whip up an eggs benedict. The smell of sizzling bacon wafted through the air and succeeded in rousing her host from his slumber.

Rubbing his eyes and slowly sitting up, Otto looked over at Stella, goggle-eyed. "Pleased to see me, DV?" He blinked, vacantly. "You're calling me that, now?" The corners of his mouth started to curl upwards. Stella mirrored his gesture, returning the sheepish grin with her usual radiant glow. "You'd better be quick if you want your eggs benedict. I'm feelin kinda hungry enough for two, you know," she explained, flashing a cheeky grin at him. He had to admit, even though she had slept in her clothes and obviously hadn't had the opportunity to freshen up, she still managed to look damn impressive.

"Now this is just unreal. How do you know I like eggs benedict?" he asked her. "I don't, she replied. But I like them!" He had to chuckle to himself. She blended charm, amiability and deadpan humour into one potent cocktail. Standing up and walking across to her, he held out his arms, inviting her embrace. "Thank you for looking after me last night, by the way. For all I know, you could have emptied my apartment whilst I slept right through it!" As soon as the words left his lips, he realised too late how it must have sounded - as though he was suggesting that she might have been some common thief and not the remarkable woman he was enjoying getting to know. Before he could temper his words and start to make excuses, to his great relief, Stella let out a good natured laugh and from her eyes, he could tell that she had not taken anything the way he had feared.

They embraced with genuine affection. Otto considered leaning in for the kiss, but found himself paralysed with indecision. Sensing this, Stella released him from his torment and snapped back into her tasks, continuing to ready their breakfast. Anticipating a potential awkward silence, Otto took no chances and "Here. At least let me grab the orange juice." They buzzed around the kitchen, he making awkward, clumsy movements, she making practised, graceful movements.

Within a short time, they found themselves at the table, both ravenous with hunger and making short work of the breakfast which Stella had expertly prepared. Otto brokered the conversation. "Sorry that I fell asleep before I could really show the capabilities of my system. To tell you the truth though, it's not quite the finished article yet. It's just in beta mode right now, meaning that it works well enough and you can feed basic queries into the machine, but the finished article is a little way off." Stella interjected "that's OK. From what you described, it sounded pretty awesome. I'd love an in-depth demo when it's ready." Otto beamed at this. "Deal!"

A slight unease spread over her as it became apparent that he was totally unaware of the questions she had fed into the machine whilst he was sleeping. To all intents and purposes, she had no real grounds for feeling guilt other than the possible suggestion that she should maybe have waited for him to wake up and asked his permission. The reality was that she just couldn't contain her curiosity and felt an urge to ask questions.

Before she could share her thoughts with him, it was time to head out and to get the day's work underway. She would have to make a diversion to her apartment en route to her office and in any case, she was going to be late. It would be necessary to call her boss and come up with some subterfuge. She really hoped he would buy it and therefore spare any possibility for gossip to ensue from the disruption to her normal punctuality.

Otto missed his regular jog that morning for the first time in months, but on this occasion he felt he could grant himself a pass. As they rode the elevator down to ground level, he came out with an unusual statement of confidence. "I want to see you again. What are you doing tonight?" Stella's natural confidence temporarily deserted her. As she struggled to summon a response which carried the correct measure of allure and gentle pushback, Otto got there first. "Meet me at Acquerellos, 7pm." With that, summoning his inner James Bond, he walked off nonchalantly, leaving Stella behind him at a loss.

She called after him. "You're crazy. No-one can get a table at Acquerellos on the same day." Smiling whilst staring straight ahead, he called back over his shoulder "friends in high places." Grinning like a Cheshire Cat, he turned the car and flagged down a cab. He had to get back into the office and show his face. Appearances were the order of the day. Besides, he had a major favour to call in if he was going to secure a table at one of San Francisco's finest eateries.

Chapter 8

It was a hot and humid evening in Singapore and Trang was just getting started with working his charms on the latest girl in a cocktail bar in Marina Bay. His phone pinged. Sighing at the unwelcome distraction, he glanced down at his phone and saw that it was a WhatsApp message from Otto. "Just a second," he said to the half distracted girl sitting at the bar.

Need to get your eyeballs on something. This is unreal.
OK, but does it have to be now?
Please.

Making his excuses with more than a tinge of regret, Trang pulled himself away from his latest prey. Luckily, his office was close by and using his 24 hour key card, he entered the building and stepped less than 15 minutes later into his office. Unable to shake a lingering sense of mild resentment at having his evening interrupted for the purposes of talking shop, he opened up his laptop and kicked off a video conferencing session with his friend on the West coast. "This had better be good, man. I've just left a nice young girl unattended at the bar for you." Chuckling at this comment which was so typical of his Lothario-esque friend, he pressed ahead. "Oh, you're going to *love* this, Trang old buddy. Well worth a brief diversion." Checking first to ensure that his connection was running through a secure virtual private network, Otto shared his screen and quickly brought Trang up to speed on where he had got up to.

The process of assimilating the sheer scale of his friend's achievement in such a short space of time caused Trang to issue a series of exclamations in his inimitable way, the timbre of his diction punctuated by irregular squawks and hollering. Otto had no idea as to the meaning of the words his friend uttered, but he had grown used to such peculiarities and waited patiently for Trang to regain his former composure.

Once he had collected himself, he ventured a few confused questions with a view to making sense of it all. "But we were only speaking the other day...? How was it humanly possible? You *must* have had some help somewhere." Otto responded by slowly shaking his head from side to side, a wide beam spreading slowly across his face as he did so. "No man. I didn't even need drugs to keep me awake as I tunnelled through the night. Not unless you count espresso, that is."

"Sweet Jesus," declared Trang, still in a state of disbelief. "And this thing *actually* works?" Otto was only too happy to offer his friend a demonstration. The two young programmers then spent the next 20 minutes discussing a range of valid and actionable scenarios, both real life and hypothetical, then fed them through Otto's working template. The computer's suggestions were revelatory and brought to mind IBM's all conquering supercomputer *Deep Blue* which became the first computer in the world to beat a reigning chess world champion, in this case Garry Kasparov. That event laid down a marker in the evolution of artificial intelligence and demonstrated the significant ground it was making up on human intelligence.

Brute computational force enabled *Deep Blue* to evaluate millions of positions in the blink of an eye and whilst Otto's tool borrowed heavily on that concept, his new innovation also relied on the concepts of neural networks and reinforcement learning to fine tune its abilities even further.

Allowing the information to soak in, Trang then began firing deep and complex questions at his friend in a bid to understand exactly what algorithms went into the wiring of such a machine and perhaps more importantly, how did he arrive at deciding which factors to base them on? Otto cited something called the *Theory of reasoned action* which aims to explain the relationship between attitudes and behaviours within human action. Developed in the late 1960s, the hypothesis is mainly used to predict how individuals will behave based on their pre-existing attitudes and behavioural intentions. An individual's decision to engage in a particular behaviour is based on the outcomes the individual expects will come as a result of performing the behaviour.

"That is ingenious. Simply brilliant. I have to take my hat off to you, DV. This is next level stuff you're playing around with here, you know." Otto's chest swelled with pride. Naturally, he was content to earn the big bucks, enjoy the attention from attractive girls and be able to buy pretty much whatever he wanted but the one thing that mattered much more to him than any of that, was recognition.

When it came from colleagues, bosses or industry professionals, he was gratified, but when it came from a close friend and someone that he considered a genuine peer, it meant a lot. It was clear from the look of wonder on Trang's face that he genuinely was impressed with the work he'd accomplished so far. He decided to further place his confidence in his friend. "You know, Trang. You're the only one who really knows about this. The only person who *gets* it." His friend's countenance glowed with pride. "Then I feel pretty honoured that you're taking the time to show it to me. Who knows? Maybe it was worth walking away from a sure thing at the bar tonight," he laughed. Otto joined him in his good natured laughter.

"So what's next, man?" Otto rubbed his chin suddenly. Actually...I still haven't decided. I guess I'll keep working on expanding the core functionalities, polishing up the user interface and then getting it bug tested. I've not thought ahead any further than that."

Trang's expression changed into one of thoughtfulness and he raised his eyes to the ceiling in momentary contemplation. "You do know that this thing, if you're first to market with it and you do it properly, it could make you richer than Jeff Bezos, right?" "Sure," replied Otto. "But I'm not in this for the money. If something like this could solve real world problems and anticipate crises before they reach the critical stage, maybe I'll have helped to make the world a slightly better place." Trang let out a derisive snort. "You Americans!" A snicker was followed immediately by another obscure Vietnamese expletive.

"I'm just saying, man. It's easy to be seen as a hypocrite in this business, right? Yeah, the money, the cars, the investor parties, the private jets - all very wonderful and for sure, nice work if you can get it. But there has to be more to life than just material possessions. Surely?!"

Otto could see pretty quickly with one look at his friend's bemused expression that he was fighting a losing battle in trying to convince him of any lifestyle other than the extravagant and lavish one to which he was well accustomed. Trang shook his head in a mock show of bewilderment that seemed to say 'there's no helping that guy!'

He attempted to clarify his position. "Look, DV. You're a good guy. One of the best. I admire your moral principles greatly. That's not to say that you wouldn't benefit greatly from some R&R over here in Singapore, but that's for another time. I'm sure we can get you loosened up another time. As far as this project goes, you're definitely onto something here, man. If I can help in any way, you know where I am."

Otto felt very happy to have such a good friend to lean upon. "Thanks, man. You're a gentleman *and* a scholar." "OK, laters," replied Trang hurriedly, with a somewhat rushed thumbs up to the screen before hitting the red button. Otto had the impression that he might well be on his way back to the casino to track down the young girl who had earlier slipped from his grasp.

Suddenly the room was still. Enjoying the peace, he glanced out of his window down toward the marina at Pier 40. It was shaping up to be a beautiful day and scores of kayaks could be seen scattered across the bay, their occupants paddling them with enthusiasm across the glistening dark blue waters. Remembering with a jolt the favour that he desperately needed to come through, he picked his phone back up and dialled someone that definitely owed him.

"Call Jimmy Sands," he commanded of his phone. 'Calling Jimmy Sands. Mobile,' came the obedient reply, with pleasing efficiency. After a few rings, a deep, booming voice answered with genuine warmth. "DV! How are you, my man?" The owner of the voice was a technical support manager who Otto liked and respected in equal measure. A bear-like man mountain who hailed originally from Canada, Jimmy was as amiable as they came and was seen universally as an avuncular character to those who worked both underneath and around him. Otto had gotten him out of a jam the previous year when a particularly difficult customer raised hell about an unresolved technical problem, which wasn't getting any better and was frankly, getting out of control.

Jimmy in normal circumstances being the cool head whilst those around him were busy losing theirs, even found himself sinking into ever greater difficulties with the customer in question and when it seemed at the 11th hour as though they were going to lose the client, Otto managed to swoop in and save the day.

He did this by working closely with Jimmy to diagnose and troubleshoot the problem. Where the entire technical support organisation had been unable to fix the problem, Otto simply found himself a quiet booth and wrote some highly inventive code which, using terrific imagination, managed single-handedly to save the long standing relationship with the client and earn him a major favour to hold in store for a future occasion such as this one. The reason Otto came to Jimmy on this one? It just so happened that Jimmy was very good friends with the owner of Acquerellos.

"Ah, come on man! Are you nuts? Even I won't be able to get a table there tonight. They've got a 3 week waiting list for chrissakes!" Embarking on a lively and passionate rant, the sheer volume of his broadside was enough to distort the speaker of Otto's mobile phone, so much so that he was forced to hold it away from his ear and simply wait, having no other option than to wait for the Canadian to cool down.

Spotting a sliver sized gap in the conversation, Otto dived in, adopting a nonchalant tone. "That was a pretty big headache for you wasn't it, pal?" He casually dropped in the name of the client that came within a whisker of forsaking their organisation for a rival. He could have sworn that he heard Jimmy growling under his breath, wrestling petulantly with this seemingly impossible moral dilemma. He pictured him sitting in his great big leather chair, splenetic in mood, taking a pencil between his fingers and unconsciously applying pressure to that object.

Otto was, in a sense, taking advantage of his friend here. He knew well that Jimmy was an honourable guy whose integrity would always lead him to try and do the right thing for someone. It just took a semblance of gentle manipulation, that was all. Besides, he really needed the guy to come through. He didn't want to look a total fool in front of Stella. Not when he was trying his level best to win her. Cautiously and at length, the indebted party calmed himself down and agreed to reach out to the restaurant owner. Otto thanked him effusively and quietly hoped for the improbable.

Less than 20 minutes later, he received a message via WhatsApp.

Booked you and the unlucky lady a table for 2 at 7.30pm. Consider the favour repaid, asshole. Don't screw it up. Good luck. JS.

Otto couldn't help himself and he let out a great laugh which was borne of both relief and gratitude to the big Canadian. Wandering out to the spacious kitchen down the hall to make himself a cup of Earl Grey tea, he briefly made small talk with a handful of colleagues and acquaintances before heading back to his office to resume Project Ignoto.

Across town at that very moment, Jennifer and Stella were sitting on a bench in Mission Dolores Park, admiring the spectacular views of the city's skyline. Confiding in her friend what she imparted from the conversation with Otto prior to his falling asleep and what she subsequently gleaned from his laptop as he lay slumbering, she shared the strain of her moral dilemma about whether she ought to tell him what she knew or whether it was better to simply keep it to herself. Jennifer had a number of questions for her. "Back up a second, sister. Are you telling me that your guy has developed a system that actually makes momentous decisions on behalf of humans?" Stella nodded. "Pretty much," she conceded. "That this system can more or less do the job of hostage negotiators, judges, presidents, police chiefs etc?" Another nod in the affirmative. "Unreal," she said, weighing it all up.

Jennifer took a moment to plot out her next question. "What's the worst that could happen? If you came clean, I mean?" Looking at her, Stella fought to resist an incredulous expression from colonising her face. "I could lose his trust? It could all be over before it's started." These sentiments were all conveyed directly from the heart and it showed. In a misguided effort to lighten the mood, her friend attempted a joke. "Plus, you'd miss out on the opportunity to dine at Acquerellos."

Jennifer received a sharp jab on the upper arm for her troubles. "Ow! *Someone's* sensitive!" "Sorry," retorted Stella, seemingly anything but. "If you want my advice, finish work early today. Make whatever excuse you need to. Get yourself home at a good time, allow enough time to take a long shower and make yourself look totally stunning! He won't be able to resist you. That I am sure of, honey." Having dispensed this advice, Jennifer crowned her guidance with a conspiratorial wink. The wind rustled gently through the trees as the dappled sunlight shone airily on the ladies' faces. Children played nearby and a competitive tennis match between a father and son was in full swing in the middle distance.

Stella seemed to have reached a new inner clarity granted as a by-product of healthy fresh air, thinking time and the sage advice of a close friend. Patting Jennifer softly on the thigh, she made a suggestion. "Come on, let's go grab a coffee."

Meanwhile 400 miles south in a seedy Los Angeles neighbourhood consisting of squalid bedsits and warring gangs, a particularly nasty attack dog was about to be unleashed on an unsuspecting victim. An untraceable mobile phone rang. A voice answered in Russian. "This is Station Voronezh. Identify yourself." The receiving party duly complied. The caller then demanded answers to a series of questions, the purpose of which was evidently to confirm beyond any doubt that they were indeed speaking to their LA based asset. The due diligence and assorted formalities eventually satisfied, the caller got down to brass tacks and set out the parameters of the mission with which the agent was about to be tasked. The instructions were delivered with strict and impersonal coldness.

"Pay attention and listen carefully. You will receive an encrypted email. Enter the following password: drozdz1989USSRmidav. Open the email. You have a maximum of 5 minutes to read the report, absorb and memorise the content contained within. It will permanently delete itself after exactly 300 seconds. All functions for copying, pasting and screenshotting of any kind is disabled." The agent acceded to these dry, hard-edged instructions. Before you proceed to open the email, I will now provide you with a high level overview.

The target for acquisition is an American computer scientist named Otto Delvechhio. We believe his nickname is "DV." He's 23 years old and occupies a high position in America's high tech industry in spite of his age. We have evidence to corroborate our suspicion that he has successfully developed a beta-stage machine learning application which could represent a threat to Russia. We want you to get close to this young American. You will pose as an experienced career executive head-hunter. It is paramount that you are convincing and manage to gain his confidence. Credibility is of the utmost importance. We hear that the American regularly turns down the advances of the world's most attractive companies to remain loyal to his employer, *Camarillo Tech*."

A flicker of admiration sparked somewhere within the agent's stomach. He looked on with favour those who displayed unwavering loyalty, whether it was to their flag, their employer or their spouse. He loathed betrayal more than anything else. However, he was also a past master at hiding his true feelings and held fast to the idea that he was a professional. Duty had no sweethearts and to remain focused on the job in hand was the key to accomplishing any mission with which he was entrusted.

The commanding voice resumed its discourse. "You will be known as Vadim Drozdz. No change in age - you remain 31 years of age. We will issue you with the commensurate items of clothing and personal effects necessary to maintain the required appearances. Is everything understood? Agent Drozdz answered in the affirmative and the call was terminated. Swiftly removing the sim card from the untraceable phone as he had done many times before, he took the phone out to his yard and dropped it into a steel incinerator before spraying liquid petroleum over the condemned handset and setting it alight. Within 5 minutes, there would be no trace of the mobile ever having existed.

The neighbourhood in which he was currently situated was less than salubrious and he was looking forward to escaping that place and heading for newer surroundings. They couldn't be much worse, he figured. A gunshot went off in the vicinity, followed by a blood-curdling scream. Chaos and a general commotion ensued and it wasn't long before the surrounding streets were crawling with police cars. The accumulated sirens wailed like distressed new-borns. Drozdz went back inside the bedsit to escape the noise and the baking hot sun.

Born in Russia to Polish parents, he had been posted to all corners of the globe on various assignments, yet had never really become comfortable in hot and humid environments, this one included. Sinking down into the decrepit sofa in the trashed living room, he readied himself for an intense burst of concentration which would oblige him to utilise his considerable powers of visual recall to memorise the finer points of his impending mission. Undergoing a series of elaborate stretches to clear his mind, he leaned forward and typed in the password to unlock his ordained objectives.

300 seconds elapsed and the screen's composition changed without warning from a simple text document to that of a featureless grey canvas. Drozdz smiled to himself. It was like child's play. He was going to enjoy this mission a great deal. Whilst not in the same league of brutality as Yudashkin, Drozdz had a callous streak of his own and if given an order to terminate someone or something, he would always choose unquestioningly to follow the wishes of his superiors.

The instructions he had received via his 5 minute brief were clear. He needed to leave his current location and leave everything behind, before heading downtown to catch a greyhound bus to San Francisco. A large sum of money would be wired to him via an escrow, which upon arrival in the city, he would collect from a branch of Western Union just off 7th street. The same sum would be loaded onto a prepaid Mastercard to avoid the likely suspicion that accompanies spending large volumes of cash. That task completed, he was required next to head to an Airbnb which had been rented in his chosen name for one month, paid up in advance. From there, he would head to the Armani store on Grant Street to populate his wardrobe with the appropriate sartorial additions required in order to pose as a top head-hunter.

It was time to go. Adopting a convincing American accent, he called a taxi the old fashioned way. The operator informed him gruffly that there'd be a surcharge if he wanted picking up from *that* address! Notwithstanding the fact that he was more than capable of looking after himself - being proficient in Aikido - he still preferred to pay the toll charge than walk through Skid Row, with the ever present threat of random knives and guns. Brooding over these lamentable thoughts, he waited patiently for his cab to arrive.

Chapter 9

It was a beautiful evening in the Golden Gate City. Spring had sprung, the sun was shining and a fresh explosion of greenery had spread its welcome vernal influence across the landscape. A pleasant and gentle breeze offered cool respite for those who found the heat a fraction too warm. People appeared outwardly happier and more relaxed than usual. Jackets were slung casually over shoulders, pretty summer dresses were on display and children hopped, skipped and jumped. The evening carried that unique feeling of hope infused with possibility, that sweet open-ended promise that was exclusive to all early stage relationships in the first flushes of romance. It inherently carried that joyful expectation that the future would be what you made it - everything was pure and unsullied. Any bad habits on the part of your prospective new partner had neither yet been revealed nor discovered.

There was an intangible sense of magic in the air and he was looking forward with child-like anticipation to his evening with Stella more than anything he had looked forward to for some time. With one eye on the rather swanky establishment they would be dining at tonight, he had taken care to dress smartly, but stylishly. He could still scarcely believe that his friend Jimmy had managed to secure a table for him. There was no clue as to how his friend had managed to swing it, but he cared not. All that mattered tonight was to enjoy a special evening with this enigmatic girl who held such a deep fascination for him. Standing in front of the mirror, Otto puffed his chest out with pride at the thought of taking such a remarkable woman out to dinner. Maybe Trang was right - perhaps he needed some R&R after all.

Natural shyness aside, Otto knew how to dress well and could afford to do so. Sporting a pair of navy blue chinos, a crisp and freshly laundered white shirt underneath a stylish grey Ted Baker jacket, the ensemble completed by a pair of recently polished tan leather Loake brogues, he looked the part. Dabbing a few splashes of Issey Miyake around his neck, he ran some pomade through his thick, dark hair to complete his preparatory routine. Alerted to his buzzing smartphone whose vibrations signified the near arrival of his Uber, he clasped his hands together in front of the mirror, started straight at the tense looking figure reflecting directly back at him and spoke under his breath, entreatingly. "This it, Otto. Don't screw it up." Gathering up his items, he left the apartment and rode the elevator down to the lobby. Skipping energetically down the outside steps, he leapt into the waiting taxi which was stationed outside his apartment building. The driver, who was originally from Ecuador but had immigrated to the US almost 30 years ago, was friendly and immediately engaged him in bright conversation.

"You look very smart, mister. You going somewhere nice?" He had a wholesome, trustworthy look about him. His searching brown eyes shone placidly out of a weather-beaten, wizened face. He had an aura about him which spoke of quiet acceptance, as though he'd had a hard life, but saw no purpose in complaining about it. "Sure am. Taking a lady out for dinner. First date. Well...second date actually. Sorta." The man from Ecuador smiled a wistful smile at his passenger and shook his head in a nostalgic manner. "Ah. Young love. I remember taking a very special lady out for dinner when I was a young guy, just like you are now." He made a few slight adjustments to his posture as if he was preparing to wax lyrical on a golden time long past. "I had been living in this country for just 2 years at that time. I didn't have much money, I was living hand to mouth, but I was happy enough you know?" He glanced up at his rear view mirror as if to seek confirmation from Otto. Duly supplied, the Ecuadorian continued with his recount.

"Well, one night I was out looking for fares. There weren't too many people looking for a ride, so I was about to give up and drive home when I saw this girl walking along the street. Man, she was stunning. I had never seen a girl as pretty as her before that moment. I struggled to keep my eyes on the road, you know what I'm sayin'?" He shook his head slowly from side to side, the memories all flooding back to him quite visibly.

"Anyway, I didn't notice at first, but she was being followed by these two guys. They looked like they were up to no good. I didn't like the look of them." The man's face had darkened as his memory bank supplied his mind's eye with a pictorial recall of the two aggressors. "I figured pretty quickly that she was being harassed by these two guys - something didn't look right to me. Against my better judgement, I slowed the car down and called out to her out of the window. 'Hey, lady. Are you OK?' She looked distressed and didn't seem to hear me. She just kept walking." The driver's evocation of this unfolding story was attention grabbing in its own right. "One of those two guys - who didn't look too pleasant to me - suddenly shouted at me to get the hell out of there and to mind my own f**ing business!" The man's eyes widened as though he had been teleported right back to that frightening moment in time. He nodded as if finding himself back inside that vivid reverie.

"You can imagine that I was frightened as these guys looked dangerous, and even now, I still don't know where I found the courage, but a sudden feeling of chivalry just came over me and I started shouting at the girl again. 'Hey! I'm a cab driver. Get in! I'll get you away from these guys.' She looked up at me, wide eyed like a rabbit caught in headlamps. I guess she figured she had no choice but to take a leap of faith with me. I leaned across and opened the passenger door pronto. Just as she was getting in, one of the two guys who was following closely behind caught up with her and put his hand on the door to block her path.

I'll never forget. The woman jumped out of her skin and pleaded with him "please just leave me alone." The guy was wearing grubby jeans and a white tank top stained with oil, or something. He wore a gold chain, he was covered in tattoos and had a swarthy face, kind of like mine. What did the guy do as she pleaded with him? He started laughing at her, the sonofabitch. He enjoyed every second of her discomfort. Then the guy started touching her face. She drew away from him and I just couldn't sit there and watch anymore. Seizing this feeling of courage, I reached under my seat and threw open my door. One thing my uncle back home taught me - always carry a weapon and bring to the battle, an element of surprise."

Otto remained enthralled by this old storyteller. "Just then, the other guy reached the car and started becoming even more cocky and aggressive. The girl let out a scream. I knew it was risky. There were two of them and they could have been carrying a gun. Even so, I felt that I had no option. It was time to brandish my weapon. Roaring at the top of my voice, I yelled at the two guys 'You get the hell out of here, right now. I'm not joking around.' They both stood stock still, stunned at my audaciousness, mouths agape. When I hoisted my baseball in the air and proceeded to swing it around, their expressions changed. I had the impression they were probably unarmed after all.

Their confidence deserted them and the colour drained from their cheeks. 'Hey! You wanna play rough? I'm gonna show you rough!' Charging at them, I felt like I was possessed by a demon. I felt no fear. They scattered like cats in an alleyway, man. I never saw anything like it. I must have chased them for half a mile, I dunno. Anyway, I shouted something after them and walked quickly back to my cab. The girl was still there crouching beside the car - she hadn't run away. The look in her eyes of pure relief will never leave me, man. I just asked her if she was OK and held out my hand to her. She took it, stood up slowly and I helped her gently into her seat. He exhaled deeply and looked in the rear view mirror. "And you know something, mi amigo? To cut a long story short, that special lady is now my wife. We have been married for over 20 years!"

Otto, still spellbound at the man's lucid narration, gulped in spite of himself and looked in admiration at the driver. "That is unbelievable man. A real story of the knight in shining armour rescuing a damsel in distress."

The man from Ecuador rubbed his neck sheepishly and continued. "Thanks, man. I'm happy to share it with you. You know, I still remember what went through my head in that moment just before I grabbed the baseball bat from under my seat. I thought to myself "This is it. This is the moment where I die. I escaped from all that poverty and hardship back home, only to reach America and end up dying in the street. Yet I have no regrets. You have to stand up to bullies. You must never let them win." "A-MEN," replied Otto in solidarity. The two men caught each other's eye in the mirror and suddenly broke out in an enjoyable and good natured laugh.

After their shared mirth had dissipated, the driver continued. "For years afterward, I kept looking over my shoulder when I went about the city for fear of seeing these guys again, but the crazy thing is that I never did." His voice tailed off as he floated off on another cloud of wispy remembrance.

At that moment, the taxi pulled up outside Acquerellos. Situated inside a converted chapel, this was one of *the* premier culinary experiences in the city. Offering up exquisite Italian cuisine in conjunction with an extensive wine list which read like an embarrassment of riches, getting a table here was like trying to request an audience with the pope. Hence, he felt highly privileged to be dining here tonight with a girl he felt increasingly besotted with.

As if by magic at that very moment, she arrived. His heart skipped a beat. Stella was dressed in all-white and looked dazzling. She walked toward him, flashing her radiant smile. "You look incredible." She took the compliment gracefully with a ever so slight flutter of her eyelids. He wasn't sure whether this had been meant as an ironic gesture or indeed how to react, when she grabbed his hand and exclaimed "Come on, handsome. Mustn't keep them waiting." They entered the restaurant and were immediately cocooned inside the restaurant's classy interior; the lights were pleasantly dimmed, insouciant jazz played and the sumptuous soft furnishings all conspired to lead to an impression of quality and luxuriance. Otto gave his name and they were shown to their table.

"I won't ask how on earth you got a table here at such short notice," said Stella, playfully. "If I told you, I'd have to kill you," smirked Otto in reply. Two leather-bound menus were placed discreetly on the edge of the table by a semi-invisible waiter. Stella reached across the table and put her hands on top of his. Gazing into his eyes affectionately, Otto then returned the favour and inwardly marvelled at the soft touch of her smooth, fragrant hands. The mere touch of her skin made him feel all at once reassured, serene and as though he might be able to close his eyes and drift off into a tranquil sleep.

Feeling increasingly awkward under her gaze, he searched for something, anything to break the ice with. "Thank you for breakfast the other day, he blurted out, instantly feeling a tad foolish. "Oh no problem. Eggs benedict is my party piece," she replied, wryly. Otto laughed nervously. "I can't believe I fell asleep when you came to my place." Confidence faltering, he awkwardly added "especially when it was getting interesting." Stella flicked her hair back and looked directly at him. "You stay awake for the other girls though, right?"

Spluttering like a faltering engine and trying to grope his way out of the rabbit hole he had dug for himself, he attempted to rescue the evening and recover from his edgy start. "There are no other girls. What, are you kidding me?" Putting his best puppy dog eyes on display, he looked pleadingly at her. Breaking into a smile that put his mind at rest, she put his mind at rest. "I'm only kidding. Man! You are too easy!" Instantly, he relaxed and all felt right in the world once again. He tried a different tack. "I guess I'm just nervous. Where's that sommelier?" A discreet nod brought the wine steward over to their table momentarily.

Learning that the restaurant's extensive selection was predominantly focused on the Piemonte region, they were happy to go along with the Sommelier's recommendation, which upon tasting was to Otto's taste, exquisite and a level above any wine he had ever previously sampled. Stella let out a little squeal of excitement upon learning that the restaurant had not one, but two Michelin stars bestowed upon it. Following guidance on the expert pairings for their chosen wine, Stella selected the grilled firefly squid with broccoli and saffron consommé whilst Otto plumped for the baked buffalo milk ricotta with summer squash, cherry tomato and basil.

Being a high end establishment, the management had guidelines in place which politely requested patrons to stow away their smartphones for the duration of the meal. Despite the nature of their daily work as modern professionals, they were only too happy to comply and to be free of constant distractions if only for a precious couple of hours. The selection process having now been completed, they settled down to enjoy their quality time together. "How's your day been?" ventured Otto. "I met with my friend Jennifer for coffee either side of a pretty standard day in the office," reported Stella. "One of our clients in Africa is experiencing a major shitstorm and we've been asked to handle the fallout.

Just a standard day in our field," she said, matter-of-factly. Otto, alerted to something in the vaults of his memory, ventured "not President Mbagwe? "I can't really say." "One of the most corrupt leaders on the entire continent? Let's not forget, that's up against some pretty stiff competition as well." Stella's facial expression was neutral, evidently well practised from facing endless questions from the media over many years. "You're pretty clued up, DV. What gives?" He responded with a quiet snort. "I subscribe to a global daily news digest, you know. I heard about the orders this guy gave. The way he treats his own people." Shaking his head in disgust, he sought to change the subject with as little friction as possible. Seeing his overt disdain for the client her organisation had been commissioned to smooth matters over for, she beat him to it. "Anyway, you don't want to hear about boring old me! Let's talk about you. How is your side project going?" Shrugging off his thoughts on the African dictator and quickly recovering his former balance, he brought her up to speed.

"I'm super excited. I think the building blocks are in place now. Sure the user interface is a little messy and the functionality could be greatly expanded and developed, but the key point is that the basic functionality is in place and as you saw yourself, it *actually works!*" She was quick to declare her admiration and offer her praise. "It's pretty unbelievable, Otto.

You have built something genuinely life changing. I have no idea what your plans are for taking it to market or whatever, but it already looks to me like a major achievement." He felt great pleasure in hearing her saying this. It wasn't a simple case of having one's ego massaged, she really did seem to mean what she said and whilst professional praise would have been sufficiently gratifying, to receive it from a beautiful, talented and special woman like Stella simply multiplied that intensity of that feeling.

Before long, their food arrived and as expected, it was truly delicious. Although Otto certainly had the means to eat well every night of the week if he so desired, it was a relatively infrequent event that saw him dining at a top-end restaurant such as this one. He remarked to Stella that he now understood why food such as that which they were eating was so much more expensive than standard fare. It was precisely because it was so much better than standard fare. As the evening went on and the delectable wine began to disappear, the food began to take on aphrodisiacal qualities and they both found themselves hurtling with abandon into the field of sexual magnetism.

It became inexorable that they would be going to bed together that night. They paid their bill hurriedly and hastily called a cab. As they strolled out of the restaurant holding hands, Stella set Otto's pulse racing with the old question "your place or mine?" She pouted at him provocatively, almost taunting him with her sheer magnetism. Standing on the sidewalk, he couldn't hold back any longer and threw himself at her. Their lips met and they locked in a passionate embrace. Their hearts raced with passionate anticipation and only the arrival of the Uber managed to separate them, albeit temporarily.

The short ride back to Otto's abode was tortuous and filled with tension. Their shared collective pressure was only broken when finally, they crossed the threshold of his apartment. Shoving the door closed, they each kicked off their shoes, and tearing at each other's clothes, blundered into the bedroom. Thrashing feverishly in sync with each other's writhing bodies through a night of intense passion, they came together as one and cemented their new relationship with gusto.

Outside and on the other side of the street, standing on a corner directly opposite Otto's apartment building dressed in all-black, was Drozdz. His nefarious gaze was fixed on the bedroom window, behind which lay the two new lovers. A malicious scowl spread over his face. "I see you, Otto," he imparted in Russian, menacingly.

He had been standing there for some time and had observed the two incautious lovers pawing at each other as they tumbled out of the cab unnoticed. 'Contemptible people,' he thought to himself with bitter and disapproving acrimony. Satisfied that he was now familiar with the layout of the area, level of security, police presence and as a bonus, had already gained sight of his main target for this mission, he trudged off with a self satisfied air.

The contrast between this upscale neighbourhood and the inner city slum from which he had just arrived could not have been greater. There were no wannabe rappers cruising around these streets looking for trouble, at least none that stuck out. Had there been any such characters in this area, they would likely have stuck out like a sore thumb. Just one brief look around told the casual observer of the stark divide of wealth from poverty seen right across this city. Having grown up in a family which still deeply believed in the communist ideal, Drozdz found it difficult to equate the overt wealth found amongst the high flyers of Silicon Valley just 30 miles away with the never-ending cast of ragged, down-on-their-luck panhandlers and homeless people choking the streets of this famous American city. 'If these people are so clever, then why can they not fix their own social problems?' he mused to himself with feelings of disdain and anger.

Still dressed in the same inconspicuous clothes, he glanced at his watch and observed the time: 22.16. Tomorrow, he would head to the Armani store to purchase the necessary clothes. As for now, there was nothing to do but head back to his Airbnb. Stopping to cast one final glance in the direction of the apartment window behind which he knew Delvechhio and his woman were, he sneered in their direction as if to warn them that they should enjoy their peace while they still had it and with that, slunk away into the shadowy night.

Chapter 10

Golden streaks of morning sunlight teased their way through the blinds as the entwined couple awoke from their languorous slumber. Everything felt right in the world at that moment for Otto and Stella. They had finally come together, set the seal on their new relationship and both felt immensely happy at waking up together. Birds were singing, pretty, fragrant flowers were blooming and love was in the air.

Stella was the first to open her eyes. Yawning softly, she stroked Otto's chest and watched him dotingly until he stirred. Realising he was being observed, he checked himself with an imperceptible start before a warm smile of recognition came over him. "Good morning, sleepyhead," greeted Stella. "Good morning yourself!" She leaned over and kissed him seductively. "I could get used to this," he declared with a contented expression. "Mmmm, me too," she agreed. "Let me fix up some coffee and breakfast while you grab a shower," he volunteered, stretching by degrees. "I guess it's my turn, right?" She grinned at him. "I'm not about to turn down an offer of breakfast from a handsome young man." He gave her a playful slap on the backside as he slid out of the bed.

Stella lay on the bed for a few extra moments, trying to process all that happened. It had all developed so quickly. It was as if she had been swept off her feet and not put up much resistance. Had she allowed it all to go too fast? Would he become bored of her? Helping herself to a large fluffy blue towel, she wrapped it around herself and headed into the shower.

Otto's bathroom was of a modern design and came equipped with electric blue LED lights and a futuristic shower which appeared to have all the bells and whistles. She noted features such as massage jets and a rainfall head that all added to the sense of opulence. Fortunately, operating the shower was more straightforward than she had initially feared and it was incredibly invigorating, so much so that she didn't want to step out of it. Her thoughts inevitably drifted to what she knew of Otto's invention and whether she should reveal the details of her exploration after he had fallen asleep. Not only what she had seen of it, but the subsequent thoughts and fears that had come up having thought about its wide bandwidth of potential capabilities.

She knew that she was falling in love with him and recognised that she cared about him deeply. It was impossible to push down her worries about what he might be getting himself into. Her own experiences of working in PR told her that it was very easy to make dangerous enemies in your line of work. Her own boss had his own security detail around him 24 hours a day and that was considered a natural requirement. When she looked at Otto though, he didn't appear to have any such protections around him. Whilst it was true that he didn't seem the type of guy who rubbed people up the wrong way, having something as powerful as the project he was working on in his arsenal, it wasn't difficult to imagine some pretty nasty people coming to ask questions, either to have it for themselves or to prevent him from releasing it, or worse still to destroy his work.

Stella considered herself to have a kind of sixth sense in such matters - she had a nose for detecting trouble and when potentially volatile situations were brewing, whether they be political or within a business context, she knew before most others when it was time to seek the exit route. After considering the difficulties at length, she dried off and got dressed, determined to approach Otto with her concerns over breakfast.

Otto was just laying the plates on the table as Stella entered the kitchen. "Et voila!" he exclaimed. "I've opted for smoked salmon with scrambled eggs and a cappuccino to get your day off to a great start!" He caught sight of her face which obviously betrayed her underlying emotion. "What is it?" he asked hurriedly, startled by this unexpected change in her. "I need to talk to you about something," she said quietly.

Momentarily distracted, with a furrowed brow Otto slowly sank into his chair. "OK..." he said, with a rising intonation. Stella sat down opposite him. "Don't look so worried. It's nothing serious. I just want to talk to you about the other night - after you feel asleep." He looked up at her, puzzled. "What *about* the other night?" She spread her hands out and laid her palms face-down on the table as though she were unsure how to set out her confession.

"After you fell asleep on the coach, I sat for a few moments thinking about what you had shown me. When you explained about the British in WWII and the stark choice that Churchill faced in the face of continuing Nazi invasion." Otto nodded, impressed with her recall. "Well, I sat there thinking and thinking. I kept turning it over in my head. The various ramifications and what it all means. We both know how far reaching this could be if and when it gets out." She paused to try and gauge his reaction so far, but his face gave little away. He was simply listening attentively.

"Anyway, I guess at least five minutes had gone by, maybe ten and you were still snoozing on my shoulder. I wasn't able to hold back my curiosity any longer. I just *had* to try out some queries for myself." She gave him an apologetic look. He dismissed her contrition with a small, forgiving shake of his head. "So I manoeuvred you over slightly and sat in front of the laptop. Those five or ten minutes of contemplation had raised more questions than answers, so naturally I had a number of challenges to pose your machine." Stella leaned back, her eyes filling up with tears. "Otto! It tackled everything I threw at it with such lucidity, it was unbelievable.

The answers and logic were so concise, so impossible to argue against. When it visibly illustrated the flow of thought and how each potential route was considered and then eliminated or expanded upon, all at such great speed, it made me weak-kneed in admiration for what you've created." He gazed at her in wonder. "Then why the heck are you crying, Stella?" he demanded, more in confusion than with any real force. "Because I love you!" she yelled at him, across the table with an unexpected vehemence that he didn't see coming. "I don't want you to get hurt," she pleaded. Otto was struggling to process this torrent of heartfelt sentiment. As a techie guy, he was more accustomed to dealing with fixed mathematical principles of coding and clearly defined architectural frameworks. This new heady mix of feeling and fervour were still a foreign language to him.

"Get hurt? W-what are you talking about" he stammered. "No-one is going to hurt me." Fighting back her tears she shook her head dismissively. "I don't think you understand. Once this thing gets out, it's going to be dynamite. You're going to have some people that want it for themselves and then you're going to have another bunch of people who want to destroy it and never let your work see the light of day!" Otto was taken aback and considered her outburst a little dramatic. "Stella. Don't you think you're being a little....paranoid?" She visibly made efforts to calm herself down.

"All I'm saying is that you've *got* to be careful with something like this. When was the last time in history somebody came up with something like this?" '*That's a tough one,*' he thought, somewhat immodestly. He assumed an ironic air of mock urbanity. "Alexander Graham Bell with his telephone. Thomas Edison with his incandescent light bulb, maybe. Tim Berners-Lee with his curious novelty, the world-wide web?" He chuckled at his faux swagger, even more amused at spotting a diametrically opposite reaction on the face of Stella, who seemed annoyed at his apparent lack of compassion for her exposed feelings.

Offering him a hard stare, she resumed her discourse. "*You* might not be taking this seriously, but you forget that I'm in the business of public relations. I've been trained to spot how things such as this are liable to play out and like it or not, this thing is going to throw you uncontrollably into the spotlight, like it or not." Otto had to admit that she had a point. Taking this into account, he gamely conceded ground. "You might well be right. I've already told you that I'm not in this for the money or the fame.

They're very nice to have and I'm certainly grateful for what I've got, but if you're so sure that this project is potentially so explosive as to endanger my life, then perhaps I should be listening to you. What's your advice?" Stella didn't hesitate in her response. "Privacy can be more valuable than you know. If the genie comes out of the bottle, then it's going to be nigh on impossible to ever put it back." She sighed with resignation. "What I'm trying to say is that when millions of people start to associate the invention of Ignoto with Otto Delvecchio, you'll be recognised everywhere you go, the media attention will be 24/7, 365, never-ending." She looked at him soberly.

The tone in the room had changed markedly since she entered the room. Their breakfast sat, ignored and rapidly going cold on the table before them. "Take the Beatles for example. They played together for years before they struck fame, but once it arrived, they were followed everywhere, mobbed by hysterical crowds, worshipped like some kind of new deities and were completely unable to escape the frenzy that accompanied them everywhere.

Now, if you had asked John Lennon in the midst of Beatlemania whether he'd give it all up and go back to the comparative bliss of anonymity, don't you think he would have given it serious thought?" Otto ran a finger down the bridge of his nose. "It's a nice analogy, but a) there is no guarantee that what I'm working on will have anything like the same effect and b) by the same token, if I remember correctly, John Lennon came from a pretty humble background and so if returning to a life of peace and quiet meant having to give up all his wealth and stardom, to be honest, I'm not entirely sure he would have done, you know?"

Responding without pause, Stella replied. "The point I'm trying to make is that once you've gone down this path, notwithstanding the risk of attracting unwelcome attention, you might also have to deal with the unstoppable interest that comes with bringing something like Ignoto to market." She tucked her long blonde hair behind her ears. "I'm trying to look at this as if I were asked to advise a client and appraise the situation." Otto nodded.

"OK. How do you read it?" "I see a kick-ass product in beta mode. You've worked damned hard to develop it from scratch. You know your stuff. In Silicon Valley parlance, you'd be described as a *subject matter expert*. The product clearly works, without a shadow of a doubt. The target audience is of a huge scope in the sense that it's not just for governments or major corporations. You could make a strong use case scenario for individual subscribers. It would practically sell itself." "Good summary," concurred Otto.

"Now, in terms of practical steps that I would advise my own clients of in this situation," Stella began. Otto waited, expectantly. "Protect yourself. Secure the intellectual property rights. Look at registering the necessary patents. Consider white labelling the database." Otto, impressed by her lateral thinking, interjected. "Are you suggesting white labelling for commercial purposes?" "Not necessarily, although you might consider that as part of your sales strategy later on. I'm thinking more from the perspective of distancing yourself from any unwanted repercussions."

He looked at her askance. "Unwanted repercussions? In case a far flung government should suffer a bloodthirsty coup and I'm suddenly greeted by the sight of angry flag-burning rebels queuing up outside my apartment building in the hope of carrying me off to boil in a cauldron, you mean?" She couldn't help but let out a small giggle, recognising the need for a dash of levity in their discussion. A playful slap was administered to his wrist, to which he responded with a hangdog look. "Come on, DV. Eat up. This breakfast of yours isn't going to eat itself!" Glad of some respite from their rather serious conversation, he tucked in and was unexpectedly satisfied with his culinary efforts. Maybe he wasn't such a bad cook after all. He made a mental note to invest in some cookbooks when he had made it past his current intense workload. He recalled reading somewhere the advice of some hotshot Wall Street trader that cooking and playing golf were his top two ways to tune out and achieve that elusive sense of relaxation.

Snapping back out of his thoughts, he noticed that Stella was looking at him with a placid and caring look of love. Gladly, he ascertained that she appeared once again to have returned to her usual charming and breezy countenance. "What are you thinking about now?" she enquired. "About what you said," he replied truthfully. "The truth is that Ignoto, if it were being developed in an incubator lab, would now be running through the early stages of bug testing. The fact that I'm effectively doing everything myself, and in stealth mode, means that whilst I can't work at the pace of an engineering team, I do at least have full control of how the product looks and feels, what functionality it will have.

As for the go-to-market strategy, I'm not going to be able to do all that myself." Stella leapt in. "Yes, at some point, you're going to have to bring others in. But when that time comes, you can just have them sign non-disclosure agreements." Otto beamed at her, more and more appreciative by the second at how much value she was adding to what he thought was his private project. "You know what I think, Stella?" She shook her head, coyly. "I can't imagine." "I think we're going to have a lot of fun together. Personally *and professionally*." With this, he leaned across the table and their lips met, lingering for some moments. Enjoying their fresh and new-fangled couple ship, they dismissed all talk of weighty subjects for the time being and enjoyed the remainder of their breakfast.

A matter of blocks away, an iniquitous, shady figure was emerging from his Airbnb and making his way to the city's flagship Armani store as per the directives of his mission. Having already collected the generously pre-loaded Mastercard from the designated Western Union store the previous evening, he was sufficiently equipped with the funds that would be required to stock the wardrobe of his chosen character.

Drozdz cut a menacing figure as he traversed the sun-bathed morning streets, scanning as he went the faces of those who passed by, memorising the layout of the area and as per his training, always aware of his military training. He wore slashed jeans, a scruffy grey Diesel T-shirt and an army surplus camouflage jacket. Square-jawed with pale blue eyes, short blond hair and wolfish features, his looks lent him the archetypal look of a classic Russian bad guy. He was the kind of haunted soul who gave off vibes that were at once forbidding and frosty. One brief look at him was sufficient to give the impression that this was someone who was best unapproached.

He was greeted by a friendly and exuberant sales assistant upon entering the Armani store. "Hello sir! How are you today? My name is Harvey and I'll be your assistant today. You need anything at all, you just give me a holler!" Drozdz spun around and fixed the assistant with such an icy stare that he gulped uncomfortably. After holding eye contact in this hostile manner for a full 10 seconds, he simply growled "no," in response and turning on his heel, proceeded into the store in search of what he needed. The unfortunate Harvey was left holding his throat, feeling as though he had been somehow assaulted without the use of fists and trotted gingerly away in search of a more friendly customer.

It took Drozdz less than 20 minutes to complete his reconnaissance of the store and complete his purchases. Opting to head straight back to the Airbnb to flesh out the creation of his new head-hunter alter ego, he strode with purposeful, determined steps and found malicious solace in the knowledge that he would actually be operating as a head-hunter in more than one sense of the word.

Standing a short while later in front of the bathroom mirror, decked out in expensive clothes and a wristwatch that to him stank of unrestrained wealth, egotism and signified everything that was wrong with capitalism, he assumed a smug and unshakeable sense of complacency that this mission would be *too* easy, that it would in likelihood all be over before he'd even had met an expected challenge. From what he had seen of this American so far, he was weak and corrupt like the rest of them. He would take great pleasure in stealing his toy and delivering it to Mother Russia. Nodding with hubris at himself in the mirror, he had only to bide his time. A simple case of gradually winning this guy's trust and when the time was right, making his move. He surely couldn't fail. The very idea was unthinkable.

Chapter 11

Otto couldn't believe his bad luck and cursed inwardly. Having made a failed dash to slip through the closing doors of the only elevator which was anywhere near the ground floor at that time, out of the corner of his eye he spotted the supercilious Jared Fletcher striding toward him cockily. Wildly overdressed for the office and strutting across the lobby with an ostentatious manner reminiscent of a lost peacock, he smarmily addressed Otto. "In a hurry are we, young sir?" With a huge effort to disguise the deeply ingrained disdain he held for his colleague, he coolly replied "not particularly." This brusque retort either didn't seem to register with Jared or he had thicker skin than Otto thought.

He continued chattering away with inconsequential abandon. "Mr Barker mentioned your name yesterday. Oh yeah, that's right. Wanted to know where you were. Of course, *I* didn't say a word." '*I'm sure you didn't,*' thought Otto privately. Jared's hand suddenly flailed out and gave him a playful punch on the arm. "Come on, then!" Otto instinctively flinched, wondering what on earth he meant by that. Was he about to start a fight? Here in the elevator? Surely not. He stared incredulously back at Jared. "What's her name?" Otto continued to stare, dumfounded. "Or his. Hey, I'm a modern man, you know. Whatever floats your boat. Who am I to judge?" Otto's eyes flicked around as he frantically racked his brain, trying to work out how Jared could possibly know about Stella. Like an annoying fly buzzing around a slab of meat, he prattled incessantly on. "There's always a girl involved. You weren't really ill yesterday were you?" He looked at Otto with the kind of look a sceptical parent reserves for their rumbled truant child who has feigned illness to avoid going to school.

The whole thing was preposterous and he felt himself getting hot under the collar. He expelled a gust of air through pursed lips. "Jared." His colleague temporarily put a halt to his streaming flow of words and looked at him earnestly, seemingly hanging on every word rather like a dog awaiting permission to sit up and take the biscuit from his master's hand.

"First of all. I *was* ill actually. I've been working pretty damn hard on an intense project recently, believe it or not." His speech was beginning to swell in both assertiveness and volume - indeed Otto found it difficult to keep down his rising anger at the wormy, presumptive method of questioning that Jared employed. He could contain himself when the topic of conversation was solely focused on himself, but when those close to him were dragged into unsavoury speculation, that was firmly off-limits as far as he was concerned. Jared's body language started to change and he shifted uncomfortably at this alteration in dynamics. "And secondly, whether or not I'm seeing anyone outside of work is *not* and *never will be,* your business. Have some damned respect!"

Slamming his hand against the elevator wall, he surprised himself at the strength of his savage retort and immediately felt a pang of remorse toward Jared. The guy was a dick and a slime ball, but he probably wasn't anything worse than that. Jared, admonished if not humiliated, had broken off all eye contact and the elevator had become a very quiet place, save for the piped music emanating softly through the speakers at low volume. It seemed at that moment to be regaling them with a rendition of *Is this the way to Amarillo* arranged exclusively for flamenco guitar. Mercifully, they eventually reached their floor and Jared stole out of the doors the very second they opened with a confirmatory ping.

His feelings of remorse notwithstanding, Otto was glad to see him slope away. It meant at least that he could now get on with his day. An email from Charles Barker was waiting for him in his inbox. *Feeling better, DV? Hit me up when you're ready. It would be good to check in again soon.* He meditated gratefully on the fortune of having a guy like Barker in his corner. Taking a moment to send a brief but romantic message to Stella, he pushed his chair back from his desk and stood up, stretching extravagantly.

Taking off in search of strong, black coffee, he ventured from his office in the direction of the nerdery. The crowd of familiar faces turned at different intervals in his direction to offer friendly greetings and acknowledgments. "Hey, DV! How's it hanging? What's going on with you, man? Where did you get to yesterday?" It felt nice to be back in the bosom of his comrades - indeed he drew strength from their collective mental horsepower and the sheer crackle of intellectual electricity that seemed present in the air immediately above and around their huddled, untidy cubicles.

The ebullient Brad Mason raised an arm in salutation and gestured for Otto to make his way over to his workspace. Two giant-sized curved monitors wrapped themselves around Brad like protective shields and gave him a field of vision that would have made a fighter jet pilot jealous. Talking him through the latest updates to his ongoing project around alcohol tolerance levels across different individuals, Otto was impressed by his progress but felt vindicated at the same time that he was right to keep his own cards close to his chest.

The idea of having to share his concept with countless others, even in a relatively small and restricted circle, was anathema to him. These guys around him who worked in the informally known "nerdery" all had clauses in their contract which expressly forbade them from disclosing to, or discussing with, outside sources or non employees what they were working on day-to-day. Otto knew, respected and understood the need and rationale for this - the company had to protect its IP after all and nobody wants their secrets to be sold or given away, but for him, he couldn't countenance the idea of effectively signing over his baby to the company, no matter how loyal he felt toward the corporation.

That's why to his mind, he was circumventing these contractual obligations by working on Project Ignoto in his spare time. If that cost him a few disapproving comments through the odd sick day, then he figured it was worth it. So be it. His plans for the future were as yet unclear to him, but he was confident that everything would shape up in the right way.

Stella's words of caution across the breakfast table came back to him and there and then, he made a promise to himself to start sketching out an action plan centred around what steps he should consider implementing, as per her advice. Making his excuses, he bade farewell to his companions and with the prescribed mug of coffee in hand, retraced his steps to his office and began his preparation in earnest.

Down on the ground floor, a sharp suited, athletically built, young blonde haired man had just entered the building through the revolving doors. Wearing a $2,000 Armani suit, polished black shoes and an equally expensive wristwatch, he carried a black leather conference folder and made his way across the shining marbled lobby with a polished, confident bearing.

Heading straight toward the large and imposing reception desk, he slowed his pace at the sight of a dandyish middle-aged man who appeared to be engaging in a gossipy and rather unprofessional way with the receptionist who was stationed behind the bank of telephones. Leaning indiscreetly across the desk in order to whisper his sentiments to the receptionist, neither of them at first seemed to have noticed the unannounced visitor.

Straining his ears, the ever alert Drozdz tried to gather snippets of their conversation to gather vital clues as to what kind of organisation this was. To his marked surprise, he thought he heard the foppish man leaning across the reception desk utter the name "Delvecchio." Making a supreme effort to blend into the background by pretending to be reading something on his smartphone, he surreptitiously attempted to turn his ear toward the hushed dialogue which passed between the two employees in front of him.

'I've had it up to here, Annie," the man appeared to say. "That little punk Delvecchio is getting too big for his boots! Who the heck does he think he is?" Drozdz, taking full advantage of his apparent cloak of invisibility, pricked up his ears at the fortuitous mention of the target who sat at the very centre of this operation.

Offering perfunctory expressions of solidarity on the man's behalf, coupled with exclamations at the audacity of the young man who had so wounded his feelings, the receptionist realised with a start that there was a visitor waiting to be attended to. Snapping quickly back into professional mode with an aplomb hitherto unseen, the fop sluggishly followed suit and took to his feet, looking discomfited and smoothing his suit as if to hide his shame at letting his guard down in front of a visitor so carelessly. Stepping forward, the razor sharp, alert-looking young man in the $2,000 dollar suit spoke in bright tones with a vaguely foreign sounding American accent. "Not *the* Delvecchio? Otto Delvecchio? Pioneering artificial intelligence specialist?"

Fingering his tie and maintaining a distrustful, distant expression, Jared tried to weigh up whose side he ought to be on and with whom he should derive greater benefits from ingratiating himself with. He looked at this sharp-suited young business and determined that he must have money. He looked pretty young. Probably wealthy parents, he considered. Or maybe he struck gold early on. Who could tell these days? Annie broke the silence. "Yes, that's right. Otto is one of our star employees. We're very proud and fortunate to have him working here at Camarillo Tech." Flashing a beaming smile at her and showing his perfect, polar-white teeth, he replied with gushing enthusiasm. "Man, am I relieved! I've been hoping to catch up with him for some time now. I'm in town for a conference and thought I might drop by and grab a coffee with him." Evaluating the situation quickly in his mind, the politically minded Jared started to err on the side of caution and decided that he would be better placed to make a positive impression with this guy, particularly since he might turn out to be somebody worth knowing.

He joined the conversation. "DV is a very talented young man - that's for sure. So, how do you guys know each other?" Flashing the same winning smile at Jared, Drozdz replied with his carefully rehearsed cover story. "We're old college friends. Well, I say college. I guess I should use the word university, right? I was a visiting lecturer and gave talks on occasion." Jared bought it straight away. *So far so good*, thought Drozdz. "I'm one of the senior project managers here. Jared Fletcher."

He proffered his hand to the young man. Drozdz complied with a vice-like firm handshake that felt chastening to Jared. Gripping his hand without dropping for a second, that 1000 megawatt smile, Jared was glad to get his hand back if only to have the opportunity to nurse it back to health. "Nice to meet you, Jared." Drozdz was sizing him up all the time. He considered him hopelessly weak and infinitely exploitable. He considered to himself that the guy could be a useful source from which he might glean information. "Do you have an appointment with Mr Delvecchio? broke in Annie. "I'm sorry to say that I don't. This is more of a social call." Jared, ever keen to try and build an advantage, cut into the conversation. "Hey, listen. I know Otto pretty well and could always take you up to his office if you like? It'd save you some time if nothing else."

Annie, ever conscious of the standard protocols of business, which included not allowing just anybody from out on the street access to the building without a pre-arranged appointment, no matter how smart they dressed, started to raise objections to Jared's suggestion. "Well, actually Jared, we don't..." Before she could make her point, he waved away her concerns with a pompous wave of the hand and simply talked over her. "Otto and I have worked together on a number of projects and I'd like to think that we've developed a pretty close bond during his time working here." His patronising manner was fully transparent to Drozdz but he played along of course in the expectation that it would lead him to a first face-to-face meeting with his target. He wouldn't be disappointed in this regard. In fact, he could scarcely believe his luck.

The look on Annie's face was one of conflict, being frozen between deference to Jared, who unquestionably occupied a higher position within the organisation than she did but at the same time a reasonable and surely justified concern for the disregard of standard safety protocols which she had just witnessed. The flagrant manner with which Jared had dismissed them in order to curry favour with a slick young businessman, seemed to her ill-advised and she strongly felt that she ought to report the incident up the chain. She figured that by turning a blind eye, she might run the risk of implicating herself along with Jared.

The two men continued their conversation in front of her desk, although it seemed apparent that most of the talking was being done by Jared whilst the young guy was simply listening and taking it all in. "DV, as we like to call him around here, has been responsible for a whole host of innovations in our R&D unit. He's a truly excellent problem-solver, an innovative thinker and an asset to the organisation." This cloying praise of Otto didn't seem to Jared in any way ironic or to represent double standards on his part. He simply waxed lyrical about his colleague as though they were the best of friends and he was his most devoted admirer. Drozdz continued to nod and smile, inserting polite interjections such as "oh really?" and "fascinating" where such responses were required.

Turning briefly to Annie, telling her rather than asking her, he simply stated "I'll be taking this young man up to Otto's floor now. Perhaps I can show you around if you have time?" Stiffening with growing annoyance at the way Jared was effectively ignoring anything she had to say on the matter, she abruptly addressed Drozdz. "May I have your name, please?" Like a sycophantic parrot, Jared echoed the question. "Oh yes, my bad. I should've asked you that. What is your name?" "My name is Vadim. Vadim Drozdz." Annie attempted to write the name down. "Forgive me, Vadim. Can you spell your last name out for me?"

He smiled at her patiently. "Sure. D-R-O-Z-D-Z." Annie scribbled out a misplaced letter and corrected it. "Is that an Eastern European name?" she enquired. "It sure is. My parents were born in Poland. We do like our zee's in Poland." With this, Drozdz let out a small and politely encapsulated laugh. Annie handed him a lanyard and ID badge to drape around his neck. "Would you mind looking into the camera just here," she requested of him, pointing her finger down at the small lens which was placed directly on top of her computer monitor.

Before he could reply, Jared, becoming impatient cut in. "Come, Annie. I don't think we need to be quite so formal for a *visiting lecturer*," he enunciated those last two words with such condescension that Annie felt her blood start to boil. Drozdz, who didn't particularly want to be captured, especially right here in the lobby of Delvecchio's company, suddenly raised his wrist and made a show of checking the time on his ever-so-slightly vulgar watch.

Seeing this action, Jared's eyes widened in a sudden panic. "Well, come along Vadim. We don't want to keep a busy gentleman like you waiting. The elevators are this way. Follow me, please." Jared ushered him swiftly away from the reception desk toward the bank of elevators. Annie frowned in exasperation after the two men. She only had to think for a matter of seconds before she decided to do something about it.

Pulling open the internal company messaging app, she opened a new window and typed a brief note for Otto. *Jared is on the way up to your office with a visitor. I don't recognise him. Eastern European last name. Very well dressed. Said that he knows of you from your college days?*

Otto, who was at that moment pulling together a task list based on the suggestions made by Stella at breakfast that morning and gathering the necessary information around IP and patents, saw the message flash up and read it with more than a smattering of confusion. Who was this visitor and why was Jared accompanying him? This guy was someone from his college days?

He puzzled over it and, drawing a blank, pushed his leather chair back, stood up and went to look out of the window. It was another sunny day in San Fran and the view out to the marina would be worth a lot of money to some greedy real estate developer, he mused. A knock sounded at his door and he spun around to see the unwelcome spectre of Jared, closely followed by his unsolicited visitor. Remembering his manners, he gave a smile of courteous warmth and gestured to the two men that they should go ahead and enter his office.

Chapter 12

"Otto, this is an old acquaintance of yours, Vadim Drozdz." Spinning round obsequiously back to Vadim to enquire of him "did I say it right?" the expensively clothed stranger spoke up with a winning grin "almost right, but don't worry - it's not an easy name to pronounce."

Jared, suddenly conscious that his bustling and fussy nature would be more of a hindrance than a help, excused himself. "Well, I'd better leave you guys together so you can catch up." Fletcher shuffled off and the two men were suddenly left alone in Otto's office. "Vadim, right?" "Yes, that's right. To tell you the truth, I'm not sure that you'll remember me." Otto looked at him carefully, trying to place him, scanning the darkest corners of his memory. "I'm sorry to say this Vadim, but I'm coming up with a blank here. You'll have to give me a clue."

Vadim smirked, giving the impression that he was enjoying this little game of charades. "Stanford," he stated plainly. "*Stanford,*" echoed Otto. Vadim tossed him a few extra little crumbs. "I was a visiting lecturer on occasion; I gave talks on the subject of the Silicon Valley mindset." "In what sense?" replied Otto. "Analysis and comparisons of the mindset of serial entrepreneurs and more specifically, what made them tick. Why they were so drawn to risk where others were not. How these people managed to build unicorn after unicorn and on almost every occasion, come out ahead."

Otto rubbed his chin, thoughtfully. "Sorry to say that I don't recall that. It actually sounds kind of interesting." "Oh it was," replied Vadim, stepping forward as if given the signal that he had secured the attention of his target. "I was commissioned to actively go out and interview top CEOs all across America, not just in the technology sector I should point out, but certainly within technology itself, is where I came across some of the most interesting people of all." Otto's interest was piqued. "Oh? How so?" Fully versed in his patter and firmly in character, Vadim continued.

"Well, on a basic level, the appetite for start-ups in other, traditional industries, such as manufacturing, the law, pharmaceuticals etc which you and I would rightly assume are ripe for disruption - the CEOs within those sectors often flagged up in my research as being far more risk-averse and traditional in their methods of thinking and decision making than their peers in high-tech." He paused to gauge Otto's line of thought. "But, things are changing. As you know, there are countless tech start-ups now pervading into areas such as agriculture, biotech, healthcare. Take farming as an example. 100 years ago, we had horses and oxen ploughing the fields manually. Now, we have drones and driverless tractors that collect expansive amounts of data that improve crop yields, enable higher quality produce and provide better guidance on how to manage food supply." Otto was visibly becoming more and more impressed with his visitor's knowledge and general awareness of the industry's direction of travel.

"Mindset is absolutely crucial to being successful in this industry," Otto concurred. "I consider ourselves - that is, the company I work for - as working right at the bleeding edge of tech. We have the privilege of working on some truly ground-breaking ideas." Vadim nodded in agreement. "Listen, how long have you got before your next meeting?" enquired Otto. "Oh, I'm not in a dreadful rush. Probably an hour or so before I have to hit the road," replied Vadim.

Always happy to have the opportunity to converse with another intellectual, he suggested that Vadim wait right there on his office sofa whilst he grabbed a couple of coffees from the machine down the corridor. Vadim happily assented and Otto left the room to fetch their hot beverages. Watching after him like a hawk and taking particular care to check whether he could be seen from any other quarters, he slowly rose from the sofa and glided stealthily over to Otto's desk.

He noticed with a flash of anger that the American had locked his laptop, negating any opportunity of making a quick screen dump let alone copy of the database. It was clear that he didn't have much time, so making a plan to be ostensibly admiring the view out of the window, he discreetly took a number of pictures of the office, using a camera pen which he would later plug into his own laptop to transfer the pictures via an encrypted network back to HQ in Moscow.

If by some unexpected twist of fate he should be forced to break in through the window, he now had enough visual clues to piece together a blueprint of the building, fire exits et al. The American's desk was tidier than he had expected that of a supposed genius's workstation to be and there were little clues as to what he was working on, with not even a notebook in sight. Growling inwardly and breathing a particularly coarse Slavic swear word, he moved away from the desk, always keeping an eye on the corridor should anyone be walking in the direction of the office.

Within a few minutes, Otto had returned to his office carrying two mugs of cafe latte. He found Vadim seated where he had left him a few moments earlier, drumming his fingers steadily on the arm of the sofa.

"Are you still working as a lecturer, Mr Drozdz?" he said, handing his visitor one of the mugs. "Please. Call me Vadim." He paused to sip his coffee. "Mmmm. That's good stuff," he opined, appreciatively. Returning to Otto's question, he gave his answer. "Not any more, no. I do get asked to give the odd *Ted Talk* but I tend to have less and less enthusiasm for public speaking these days. Any Tom, Dick or Harry can jump up on a stage and get behind a microphone these days. Same story with podcasts and blogs. How do you make your own voice heard about all the white noise?"

"It's a very salient point, Vadim," agreed Otto. "So what line of work are you in as of now?" he pursued. Vadim placed the cup gently back onto the coffee table. "Believe it or not, I set up my own search firm over in Boston a few years back. We only carry out the most confidential assignments and don't tend to broadcast our presence in the tech world, so most people haven't heard of us." Otto nursed his coffee cup thoughtfully. "So *that's* why you've come to see me." Vadim, seeing where this was going, adopted a new tone of voice, which was assertive, yet neutral. This alteration didn't escape the attention of Drozdz.

"Otto. I don't want there to be a misunderstanding. I'm not here to sell you the job of a lifetime, I'm not here to try and prize you away from this place, believe me. That's not what I'm here for." Judging by his expression, Otto appeared highly dubious of such claims. "How often do I get the chance to look up an old acquaintance and shoot the breeze on topics which are pretty much off limits to the intelligence levels of the average citizen?" Vadim said, entreatingly, holding out his hands, palms facing-up. Otto had started to fidget distractedly, as if there was something troubling him.

He appeared to be concentrating on tracing a pattern in the indents of the sofa with his left index finger. "That's just it, though. I have a pretty good memory and I just can't seem to place you anywhere. Please don't take that as a sign of me being rude or anything like that. In fact, it's driving me a little crazy not being able to associate your talks with my time at Stanford, let alone any discussions we might have had, for that matter." Vadim adopted a suitably benevolent expression, as if to say that he understood fully and that it would all come flooding back to him soon enough.

"I'm not in the least bit offended. You must remember that I was regarded as the type of lecturer who inspired fierce debate and got into plenty of intellectual sparring matches. I used to tell people that it wasn't their job to agree with me necessarily, but that they should be strong enough to stand up for something and to make their points effectively, regardless of which side of the argument they were on. Do you recall what Oscar Wilde had to say on the matter, Otto?"

Without missing a beat, Otto replied. "Of course I do! He said "I may not agree with you, but I will defend to the death your right to make an ass of yourself." "Yes!" exclaimed Vadim and broke out into what seemed like unrestrained, nonsensical laughter. Otto couldn't help but chuckle at the quotation and started to relax, reflecting on the absurdity of a stranger being brought to his office by Jared who then saw fit to underline his points by quoting Oscar Wilde.

As their merriment subsided, Vadim decided to capitalise not only on the apparent release of tension, but also the confusion he was stealthily attempting to smother his opponent with. "It might be that we have a mutual friend, although I cannot be sure." Eager to understand who that could be, he urged his visitor to divulge that information. "Trang Nguyen - does that name ring any bells?" Otto at this point started to believe that maybe this guy had featured at some point during his time at Stanford.

He seemed credible enough and sounded as though he knew his stuff. "Why - yes. He was a fellow student of mine. We studied together." "I know," said Vadim with a knowing look to match. "Last I heard, he was over in Singapore working for a major bank and earning a lot of money," continued Vadim. "Yes, he is! Not only earning a lot of money, but living the life of Riley," snickered Otto. "Well, he always was rather fond of the ladies," suggested Vadim. "That all stops of course when you get married." As he said this, Vadim tapped his fingers pointedly on the wedding ring he wore, which unbeknown to Otto, he had collected along with his money only the previous evening.

Everything was going just as Drozdz had hoped. Otto, despite a natural level of caution, appeared to be buying into the vague story of the occasional visitor to Stanford who reinforced his back story with carefully placed references to industry events and the name dropping and apparent knowledge of a close friend. His default position of not to take anything at face value was being eroded, possibly due to a lack of sleep or perhaps his increased level of vulnerability at being newly in love with a new partner. Vadim and his bosses had even paved the way to cover the likely eventuality that Otto and his immediate circle would Google his name and look into whether what he had claimed was in fact reality. A crack team of computer hackers back in Moscow had woven a complex web of fake news articles, websites, academic records and business profiles, all waiting to be discovered and taken at face value. It was as if the state had given him a brand new identity with which he could wield his influence, like a malign swiss army knife.

"Then if you're not here to poach me Vadim, what is it I can help you with?" Flashing that megawatt smile again, the shark in the sharp suit resumed his charm offensive. "I had the feeling you might ask me that." He folded his hands in his lap and fixed Otto with a look of apparent sincerity. "I could sit here and claim all kinds of bullshit stories, such as I'm here in the best spirit of networking, or I'd like to re-connect and become friends with one of the most sought-after techies in Silicon Valley, but that's not the real reason why I'm here."

Otto waited expectantly for him to elucidate. "I pride myself on my ability to read people, Otto. I know extraordinary talent when I see it. I also know that there would be little point in ever trying to persuade you to make a career move - you're not that type of guy. Loyalty is absolutely central to everything you do. Then again, by the same token, it's clear that you're not going to work for Camarillo Tech for the rest of your life." "Your point is…?" "My point, Otto, is that you are a restless creative. Your whole sense of being, sense of purpose if I might venture to be so bold, is about bringing new things *into existence*.

Things which aren't *in existence* right now." Vadim fixed him with those rapier-like pale blue eyes. Otto couldn't escape them. They were like a hypnotic whirlpool, pinning him on the spot, rendering him unable to move, let alone think outside of their current dialogue. "Some people are motivated by money. Others recognition. Others, material wealth, trophy wives, fast cars. But *that isn't you.*" Stressing each of those last three words with an almost mantra-like emphasis, Otto squirmed under his gaze, but had no means to wriggle free.

"Take those guys Jared pointed out to me. The nerds. They're paid - relatively well - to do pretty much what you're doing, at a lower level of course." Vadim leaned back on the sofa, as if to allow his words to percolate. "They feel a sense of belonging, they enjoy working in unison. But we both know the drill. Every great idea they come up with or abstract notion they are given to develop stays firmly within the confines of this corporation.

Their blue sky thinking is in effect, fenced in and it's only the senior leadership team that will derive the true benefits of those innovations." Otto replied sharply. "Maybe so, but this corporation has looked after me very well until now and those guys in the nerdery are very happy where they are." Vadim nodded patiently. "I get it. They have looked after you and quite rightly. So they should. Any number of Silicon Valley founders would give their left nut to have you in their engineering division - I know it. You know it. As I said, I'm not here to try and engineer any kind of departure." Otto looked at Drozdz intently. "Then what? What are you actually trying to say?" Vadim adopted a gaze beyond Otto, out to the forest of skyscrapers beyond.

After a few seconds, he took up his appeal once again. "You are an innovator, Otto. I read the interview with *Time* magazine last year. Your string of developments are legendary. You were described by the interviewer as a modern day Thomas Edison." Otto visibly reddened at this. "I think he was being a little generous," he shrugged modestly. "Nonsense, Otto! Credit where it's due. What I'm getting at is this." Vadim paused to adjust his cufflinks. "Let's just say hypothetically that one day you are struck with an idea which is just *too* good to share." He allowed this to sink in. Otto said nothing, waiting patiently for him to go on. "It could be an invention, an innovation or something which changes the world overnight - who knows.

My supposition is that if you were one day struck with an idea of this magnitude, there would likely be a kind of internal wrestling with your inner conscience about how you moved forward." Otto looked up to the ceiling and pondered at length. *'Where was this guy going with this? What was his agenda?'* Leveraging his best snake-oil salesman's look of faux sincerity, Vadim prepared to reveal the card he'd been waiting to lay on the table. "Here's where the sales pitch comes in." Otto had been waiting for it. He was only surprised that it had taken the guy so long to build up to it.

"Hit me with it, Vadim." Drozdz gave a curt nod before laying it out. "One of the benefits of being extremely well connected, as you can imagine, is having access to a number of other very well connected people. I'm talking about the ultra wealthy. That unique clutch of individuals who belong to the highest stratum, those who tend to stay out of the public spotlight for the most part, but have a particular interest in life-altering advancements and world-changing technology."

He glanced at Otto, studying his face for signs of engagement." The American's face gave little away, so he pressed on. "Long story short, I have privileged access to the types of people who would be willing to reward a mind so uniquely talented as yours that, well... the necessity of needing to work beyond the age of 30 would be so unnecessary as to be laughable. You could simply pick and choose any future assignments as you see fit whilst you enjoy the hard earned fruits of your labour." He observed a slight spark of intrigue in Otto's countenance. "Better yet," Vadim continued, "this would all be completely and utterly off the record. If you did decide to explore the topic of our conversation further and subsequently went on to accept a commission from one of our private investors, no-one outside of a small and select group need ever know. Not your employer, not your boss, not even the IRS."

A fine shiver that made his arm hairs stand on end, came over Otto's body, impalpable in its effect and difficult to explain, but it was there nonetheless. A sense of something shadowy and illegal was taking shape here, an embryonic elephant in the room. He felt all of a sudden conflicted by the thrill of potentially finding a viable outlet for his private work but couldn't shake the vague sense of unease at the sharp-suited, self-confident proponent who delivered the accompanying sermon, oozing and overflowing with charm. His inner discontent sat heavily in the pit of his stomach. Considering how he might approach this challenging situation if he were sat in front of a computer screen, he opted to ask a series of questions in the hope of better understanding what this all might entail.

"Is what you're suggesting in any way illegal?" he shot back. Vadim looked almost wounded. "God, no. These high net worth individuals are fully vetted and are without question who they say they are. They have commercial interests all over the world; in some cases they are self made, in others they are old-money. Through extensive checks and balances, we have been able to determine that their private investment funds are all derived from legitimate sources, such as company income, sale of businesses or stock units and in some cases, property & commercial rental income.

There are most certainly no questionable sources of income that could be traced to illegal or unethical practises." With a self-important look at Otto as if to declare '*let that be an end to such questions,*' he interlocked his fingers and rested his hands on his lap once again. Otto, however, was only just getting started with his discovery questions. "How does it work exactly? Presumably these people would wish to know a little more about me or set up interviews to find out more?" Vadim remained impassive and was prepared for the inevitable onslaught of questions. "Both sides would rightly expect full confidentiality from the outset, which is why both parties are asked to sign a non-disclosure agreement.

Think of me as the escrow in the middle, protecting both sides from any unnecessary distractions." "But what about legal protections, for example," interjected Otto. Vadim gave what he intended to represent a knowing shake of the head. "Don't worry. Both you and I know that lawyers only exist to make as much money as they can. The NDA document contains carefully crafted language to the effect that neither side will be able to bring legal challenges against the other and so by committing their signature to that document, both sides effectively waive their right to bring or face, a lawsuit in either direction."

"OK, so both parties relinquish their right to legal action?" "Correct. Both sides effectively check their weapons in at the door," replied Vadim with a smirk. *You Americans should know a thing or two about that'* he thought to himself with sour resentment. Otto stopped to contemplate. "Do I ever get to meet these people?" No," replied Vadim firmly. We assure our clients and innovators of total secrecy at all times. It just wouldn't make sense to break that promise." "It's a sensible call in my view," remarked Otto. "Another question. What happens to my IP rights?"

Vadim didn't let it show, but for a split second, he blanked on the meaning of this acronym. Luckily for him, it returned to his memory as quickly as it had vanished. "You mean your intellectual property rights," he ventured, hoping fervently that this was indeed the correct phrase. "Yes," confirmed Otto. Vadim breathed a deep sigh of relief, but took great pains not to let it show. "You retain them in full. As for the distribution of long term financial rewards - when your minimum viable product or service goes to market, we negotiate between you and the panel of private investors what sums are invested in return for a defined ownership percentage of the shell company." Otto nodded slowly. "OK, that figures. And what is your slice of the pie?"

Drozdz grinned like a Cheshire Cat and conjured up another prepared pose which displayed every one of those whitened Hollywood teeth. "I love your turn of phrase, Otto! You always had such a way with words. After all is said and done, we take 20% of the GP for the first year, 15% in year two and then 10% in perpetuity until such time the company ceases to exist." Otto let out a prolonged whistle as he computed the numbers. "Well, all I can say is that you guys must be making a lot of money." Vadim shrugged nonchalantly. "We do alright for ourselves."

Otto started to smile. "No doubt. Impressive. Deeply impressive." Vadim expressed his thanks. "So. You'll think about it?" Otto sprang up out of his seat and proffered his hand. "Yes. Yes, I will for sure. How often do opportunities like this come along." Mirroring the American's sudden elevation and shaking his hand with enthusiasm, he looked him directly in this eye. "I couldn't agree more." "Well, I'd better be going. Thanks for your time, Otto." Drozdz started to make for the door, but Otto called after him. "Wait a minute. Do you have a business card?" Reaching into his inside pocket, Drozdz procured one and handed it to Otto. It felt suitably premium in his hand and was minimalist in design with the name **Vadim Drozdz** embossed onto the front. On the rear, it simply stated Boston, MA and provided an email address & cell phone number.

"Nice business card," commented Otto. "Meh. They're kind of old hat now, but I do regard myself as something of a traditionalist," replied Vadim. Adopting a conspiratorial expression, he stopped short of the doorway and turned around. "Listen, I'll be in town for another couple of nights, then I need to go back to Boston to meet with some VCs." I don't know whether you'd like to grab a beer, or? My dollar?" He said it with such circumspection that it caused Otto to feel it would have been somewhat ungracious to decline his offer.

Digging his hands into the pockets of his chinos, he shrugged casually. "Sure, why not?" Vadim raised a thumb vertically, almost apologetically at acting in so informal a manner. "Black Hammer Brewery on Bryant Street, tomorrow at 6pm. Any good for you? "Perfect," agreed Otto. "They have a pretty good range of beers there." Projecting a relaxed grin, Vadim bade him farewell and headed off to the elevators.

Otto was left alone again to think on what had passed in this most eventful of weeks. He must have sat there for a good ten minutes before he dragged himself back to his desk. Typing in his password, he fired up his laptop and sought out Trang's contact details. Having located them quickly, he was about to call his friend when he realised that it would have been the middle of the night in Singapore and clearly too late to have disturbed his friend.

Making a mental note to call his friend later in the day, he dropped a brief SMS to Stella and returned to the tasks he was immersed in prior to receiving his unexpected visitor.

Chapter 13

Stella sent him a message that afternoon inviting him for dinner at her apartment that night. He left the office around 4pm and headed home for a refreshing shower and a change of clothes. Just before he requested an Uber, he tried to video call Trang once again. Figuring that he might just about be able to catch him before he went to bed, he was highly amused when the camera connected to display his friend with a semi-naked girl directly behind him, draping her arms around him in a rather erotic mode of interaction. "Hey, man. You do pick the worst times!"

This opening comment was accompanied by the now standard Vietnamese expletive, riddled with frustration and disbelief at his friend's poor timing. Struggling to keep a straight face, Otto replied: "You look as though you're in good hands, amigo! Nothing urgent, I'll try you again tomorrow." Ending the call without further deliberation, he snorted out loud and banged the table as a kind of affirmative salute to his far flung friend.

Riding over to her neighbourhood in Bernal Heights, he was for once, not faced with a loquacious taxi driver and enjoyed a relatively serene journey over to her ultra smart, modern apartment. Stella's home was situated on a quiet residential street attractively lined with palm trees. Away to his right, the road sloped steeply uphill toward a grassy knoll upon which sat the area's famous landmark - a microwave tower. A cloudy morning had given way to warm, agreeable evening sunshine. Stepping out of the taxi, he thanked the driver and slung a jacket over his shoulder, taking a moment to sniff the sweet smell of jasmine, which wafted through the air to him.

He noted that the adjacent building appeared to have a colourful variety of fragrant spring flowers growing in window boxes. A surge of joy and contentment shone through him. Life was good. Not wanting to keep his girl waiting, he proceeded to the door and pressed her buzzer. The miniscule video screen which was built into the wall suddenly transformed itself into life with her image. She looked staggeringly beautiful. "Hello handsome," came the greeting. Puffing out his chest, he attempted some deadpan humour. "Well, I was here to visit a beautiful young woman, but I guess *you'll* do." Rolling her eyes, Stella pressed the buzzer and granted him access.

Stepping into her stylish and generously proportioned apartment, he cast admiring glances all around the room as he absorbed the fixtures and furnishings. "Is that a *real* Kandinsky?" he asked, incredulously. "It's his work, but a copy. Gee, I wish I owned one of his originals." Placing the knuckles of his right hand under his chin, he took a closer look at the frame around the painting. "Swinging, 1925," he read out loud. "Would this style of art be classified as abstract?" Impressed even with his surface level knowledge, Stella beamed at him. "That's right. It's my favourite style." She pointed out two other paintings to Otto. "See over there. That's another Kandinsky - it was entitled *Cossacks* after the Russian cavalrymen. Look. You can recognise them from their orange hats on the right of the painting."

Otto cast an admiring glance of his own back at her. "Kandinsky believed that emotions could be expressed through the way colours and lines were arranged in a painting. He even linked musical tones to particular colours and considered colour to have a powerful spiritual impact." "Wow," exclaimed Otto out loud. Stella continued, enjoying this opportunity to share one of her passions. "That one over there is called *The Frustrated Cat* by a Spanish artist named Joan Miro." Starting to feel ever so slightly out of depth on the topic at hand, he attempted a weak joke. "The cat who *didn't* get the cream?" Raising an eyebrow in an effort to endear himself, he was met only with a quizzical look in return.

"Sorry," he said dolefully. "I don't know where I was going with that." She raised her index finger and laid it squarely on his lips with the aim of silencing him. It worked. "I tell you what we're going to do." Flicking back her hair and running her hands through it seductively, she placed both her hands on his shoulders. "We're going to open a bottle of wine, eat dinner and then you're going to take me in there." She jerked a finger over her shoulder toward the bedroom as if to underline her point. "I'm not about to argue," he declared and happily acquiesced to her commands.

Back in his Airbnb, Drozdz sent the pictures he had taken of the office earlier that day through an encrypted network back to Moscow. He sent with them a brief accompanying message. *Target acquired. Resistance unlikely. Expect IP within days.*

The message came through instantly to the control room in the rabbit warren deep below Leninsky Prospekt. Yudashkin, who survived on minimal sleep, picked up the message almost immediately. Allowing himself to register only the briefest flicker of emotion, he scrunched up the piece of paper he had been holding in his hand in celebration of this earlier than expected breakthrough. His giant hands shook as he crushed the piece of paper into a pulp, crushing as he would anyone who stood in the way of his dreams of glory and conquest. "Все крепнет и крепнет," snarled Yudashkin with venom. *Everything is getting stronger and stronger.*

A matter of hours later, aided by a fine bottle of Lambrusco, the new lovers lay intertwined in Stella's bed, basking in the lingering afterglow. Otto spoke first. "I had a visitor today in the office." "Oh?" replied Stella, half attentively. "Yeah. Some hot shot head-hunter with an Eastern European last name. Claimed that he knew me from my Stanford days. I couldn't quite place him, but I guess that's to be expected. I did come into contact with a lot of people after all." Stella didn't say anything, she seemed distracted. "So anyway, he started inflating my ego with all this spiel about how creative I was and that I was wasting my time if I planned to stay at Camarillo forever.

He then anticipated the fact that I'll always be loyal first and foremost to my employer by talking about some investment fund which the ultra-wealthy are involved in and which apparently, would remain separate from my day to day job." "What did you say to him?" Stella replied with a sleepy yawn. "I agreed to have a beer with him tomorrow night at Black Hammer on Bryant." She took this in and murmured that it was just as well since she had her Japanese class on a Thursday night. "Wanna hook up afterward?" suggested Otto. "I don't think I'll be spending the whole night with this guy." "You're sure he can't turn you?" Stella enquired, with another of her coquettish remarks. "Quite sure," he said firmly.

They lay in silence for a while longer, Stella still snoozing, Otto by now awake. "Hey, do you wanna get out of town this weekend? You know, head up the coast. Maybe spend a few days up in Napa Valley?" "Sure, she replied." That sounded pretty agreeable. "I know a great little vineyard up in Kenwood, just outside Santa Rosa." Stella drifted back off to sleep within a matter of minutes and Otto continued to dwell on the events of the previous day before eventually succumbing in turn to the dark curtain of exhaustion that closed in on him.

Back across town, Drozdz was already making plans on how he would snare Otto and force him to hand over everything he had on Project Ignoto. He had ways of getting what he wanted. Growing up in a family that clung grimly to the Communist ideal and were of the firm persuasion that capitalism and its exponents were the enemy, he'd had a whole range of unsavoury methods drummed into him from an early age. It might prove to be a chastening night for Mr Delvecchio.

A text message awaited Otto as he switched on his phone the next morning. It was from his CTO, Charles Barker. *Otto, drop in and say hi this morning. I'll be in my office between 9.30 and 10.* He greatly appreciated the avuncularity of his boss, but couldn't help but feel ever so slightly nervous. Had someone been talking or eavesdropping? Was that Vadim guy setting a trap for him in the hope of precipitating a spectacular fall from grace? All such thoughts raced through his head, before he rebuked himself and dismissed them as idle speculation. Perhaps he needed more sleep. However, he didn't mind getting less sleep if it came at the cost of fooling around with this incredible woman who lay next to him. Leaning across her prostrate form, he kissed her softly and headed across the hallway for an invigorating shower.

Plotting out the day in his mind, he formulated a mental task list. He would go and meet with Charles Barker, then he would spend a few hours accomplishing the tasks he had started around intellectual property and applying for patents. He had a series of calls he had to be on through the afternoon and then he would aim to leave the office around a quarter to six and head to his meeting with Vadim Drozdz.

Towelling off, he fixed up some breakfast for himself and Stella. Her cupboards were remarkably well stocked, so he whipped up a corned beef hash with a couple of fried eggs, before wolfing it down hungrily and heading for the door. Stella was only just dragging herself out of bed as he was preparing to leave. Departing the apartment with a lingering kiss and a firm plan to reconvene at his apartment after her Japanese class finished around 9pm, he skipped down the stairs and out the door.

Blue skies abounded in all directions and there wasn't a cloud in sight. This being a quiet, charming quarter of the city, he took the decision to stroll to the office on account of the fact that he'd dropped his jogging routine over the last few days. He figured that adding a few extra steps to his pedometer wouldn't hurt.

People on the streets appeared to be in a good mood and he observed many smiling faces as he made his way across the city; even the normally stern-faced traffic cops seemed to be in forgiving form that morning.

A quick diversion via a bookstore enabled him to pick up a beginners guide to Japanese, an investment which he hoped would pay dividends in the long run. The time was 8.25am sharp as he entered the building. Annie spotted him immediately and made a beeline for him. She waved him over anxiously, as if she were weighed down with worry.

"Did Jared bring that guy up to your office yesterday?" enquired the agitated receptionist. Otto confirmed that he had indeed. "Son of a gun!" she blurted out, swishing her left arm through the air in a show of vexation. "Why? What's the matter?" Crossly, she recounted the story of how Jared had presented himself at her desk, lounging over the counter and generally bitching and moaning about being scolded in the elevator yesterday.

"Well, Annie, he had it coming to him you know? There's only so much a person can take before they lash out." Professional enough to comment no further on the matter, her face nonetheless lent sufficient expression to how she felt about Jared to the point where no further words needed to be said.

"Well, as long as this guy is who he says he is," she summarised before returning curtly to her desk to answer a ringing phone. Otto looked after her vacantly, asking himself whether he had actually gotten to the bottom of it himself. Glancing cautiously around the lobby and scanning every square inch, he satisfied himself that the coast was clear i.e. free of his project managing colleague Jared and requested an elevator. Upon arrival in his office, he opted to go off-piste with his choice of beverage and plumped for a cup of Darjeeling with which to aid his preparations for the scheduled catch up with his CTO. 9.25am came around before he knew it. Locking his screen robotically, he slid his leather chair behind the desk and traipsed down the corridor to ride up to the 49th floor once again.

Jelinda offered him a warm welcome as he strode through to the antechamber. "Twice in a week? If I didn't know better, I'd say you must be in Mr Barker's good books." "Better than the alternative," he countered good naturedly. The door handle to the main man's office suddenly turned with a hefty clunk and swung open. "DV! Fighting fit again? Here. Catch." Without warning, Barker tossed him what looked at first glance like some miniature beanbag - it turned out on closer inspection to be a stress ball. "Now you're probably wondering why I've just tossed you a stress ball." He looked expectantly at his star player. "Right?!" Pointing to the sofa where Otto had sat on his precious visit, he gestured for the young man to take a seat. "Coffee?" "Sure. Thank you, boss." Barker waved away his deference like a kindly schoolmaster.

Both men assumed their positions facing each other, just as they had in their previous meeting. "Feeling much better, now? enquired Barker. "Much better. Must have been a 24 hour thing," replied Otto. "You know what I think, DV? Said Barker, scanning his young employee's face. "I think we're overworking you." He allowed this comment to linger. "Sir, I...," began Otto with a mind to gently protest this claim, but the raised index finger of his boss effectively cut him off. "You're an asset to the business and assets have to be carefully managed. Take baseball, or even soccer for that matter. The big hitter, the star player in effect - they need to be nurtured and deployed with careful thought and consideration.

Frankly, DV, you've been knocking them out of the park for me on a regular basis for some time now and I'm of a mind to give you some time off so that you can recharge your batteries." Otto was surprised anew at his boss' kindness and consideration of his own wellbeing and not only that of the company's bottom line. True to form, Barker then threw in one of his curveballs.

"That is unless of course, you weren't really sick and actually spent the time in front of a head-hunter, plotting your next move." Although he said it jokingly, Otto's face couldn't hide a flash of shock at this uncanny prognostication. He surprised himself with his disarmingly candid response. "A head-hunter did approach me with a proposition, but I told him that my loyalties lay with Camarillo Tech and flatly turned him down." "When was this?" demanded Barker. "Yesterday. Here in the office. Some slick Eastern European guy in an expensive suit and a chunky watch. Sounded from his accent like he had studied in the US."

Barker's brow furrowed as he digested these unexpected revelations. "What firm was this guy from?" "He didn't actually say," replied Otto. He paused anxiously. "If it makes you feel any better, he actually said that it was clear that I had no interest in leaving Camarillo Tech and that it was a waste of time trying to persuade me otherwise." Barker remained pensive. "We mustn't rule out the possibility of corporate espionage," he announced, to Otto's surprise. "Espionage?" echoed the younger of the two men. "That's right. He may not have been here to offer you a job. He might well have been fishing for information, or trying to extract sensitive data." He mused further.

"Eastern European guy, you say?" Otto nodded, watching as his boss became gripped by deep thought. "Hmmm. What have you been working on recently?" Otto's heart skipped a beat. *Surely there wasn't a possibility that his private project had come to light? He'd been so careful. Who knew about it?* It was his turn to become gripped by rumination. *Stella?* The thought hit him like a freight truck. *Stella knew about his stealth mode project. But surely...she wouldn't have disclosed this to anyone. Not after all they had been through? Then again, everything had happened so quickly. Was she just a honeytrap?*

The thought stuck in his craw, like foul-tasting poison dripping slowly down his throat. Maybe that old lecturer of his had been right in issuing his warnings of caution, despite leaving himself open to accusations of sexism. Barker was speaking to him through the fuggy haze. "Sorry, can you repeat that?" he asked, trying to expel the mists of confusion from his mind. "The last project was that one I gave an interview to Crunchbase for a few days ago. It's due for release at the end of the month." Barker stood up suddenly and walked slowly across to the tall windows which boasted one of the finest views in the city. He slipped both hands into his pockets and didn't speak for a good 30 seconds or so.

"Did this guy leave a card at all?" Otto reached inside his blazer and pulled out the card which Drozdz had given him. "He did. I've got it right here." Barker turned and marched back across the room to where Otto sat. Instinctively, Otto handed the business card over to his boss. Barker turned the card over and over in his hand, studying it as if seeking clues to aid the unravelling of some great mystery. "I don't like the sound of this, DV, I gotta tell you."

He ran a hand through his thick, greying hair. "Someone is trying to get at you. That's my gut feeling." Otto shifted uncomfortably in his seat. He didn't know what to say. Barker appeared to shift purposefully into a new, determined disposition. He flapped the business card in his hand back and forth, as though it were a lit match he were trying to extinguish, whilst looking intently at Otto. "I'm going to look into this guy. Leave the card with me for 24 hours. We'll have another chat in the morning. OK?" He wasn't about to refuse his boss' request, so demurred without protest and thus the discussion was terminated. The coffee would have to wait for another time.

He spent the remainder of his day in long, concentrated bursts of productivity, fleshing out the framework of the IP for Project Ignoto as well as filing an incognito application with the United States Patent and Trademark Office. Pausing only for a simple lunch that consisted of a BLT sandwich and iced tea, he flew through the gears and made swift progress, ticking off the tasks on his mental list as he went.

Closing his laptop at 5.15pm, he considered calling Trang once again, but realised with a notch of irritation that he had probably missed the boat for today. He sat and wondered whether his good friend would have the same girl lying next to him tonight or whether he had snaffled a new quarry in the preceding 24 hours. Who knew? Deciding instead to drop him a line, he composed a note. *Vadim Drozdz:- does that name mean anything to you? He dropped by my office today and said he knew us both from Stanford. I didn't recognise him at all. Going to investigate further over a beer. Go easy, my friend.*

Hitting the send button, he made his way down to Bryant St for the pre-arranged rendezvous with the enigmatic head-hunter. By contrast, Drozdz himself had spent the whole day preparing for and rehearsing his game plan for the evening. Moscow had earlier sent him an encrypted message which although laudatory in its expressions, remained cautiously-toned and behove him to follow their strict instructions and not to diverge nor waver from the end-goal at any time. To do so would not only be unpatriotic, but could lead to acute consequences. Duly warned, the Russian dressed himself in more relaxed, smart casual attire for the evening and checking for the 3rd time the contents of his small, brown leather holdall, he determined that he was ready. The time was 5.27pm and he had but a short walk to reach the location on Bryant Street.

Chapter 14

A popular spot with the post-work office crowd, Black Hammer Brewery was packed out when Otto arrived; people were spilling out onto the street, taking advantage of the early spring warmth and lingering daylight. Having arrived 5 minutes early, he asked the server whether a table had been booked under the name of either Delvecchio or Drozdz? The server gave him a sideways glance as he uttered the latter and he was invited to spell it out, word by word. "D-R-O-D," he began before a cry across the room was somehow heard above the din of Bon Jovi. It was Drozdz himself, waving in tandem with that charming smile of his, visually announcing with supreme confidence that he had already arrived and secured the table in question.

Dressed once again in Armani, only this time from their casual range, he looked like a catalogue model, almost too kosher to be taken as an everyday member of the public. Otto wandered over to the table, uttering various apologies for not getting there first and for making him wait. "Not at all," offered Vadim with a relaxed air, waving his hand toward the opposite chair by way of invitation. "I took the liberty of ordering a couple of beers." "That's very kind of you, thanks Vadim." "So, good day so far?" posed the Russian. "So far so good. Managed to get a few things ticked off of the list."

The two men continued to make polite conversation in this way until their server appeared with a circular tray and which stood two glasses of frothy beer. "A welcome sight, I'm sure," commented Vadim nonchalantly. "This one if I'm not mistaken is from the state of Oregon. Dry hopped with notes of guava and grapefruit." Otto took a sip of the beer in question and winced at the acidity. Vadim, seeing this, expressed regret for having gone ahead without first enquiring as to his preferences.

"I guess this style is not to your taste. My apologies for jumping the gun. Allow me to buy you an alternative beer of your choice." "You really don't have to do that, Vadim." "Please. I insist." Otto didn't put up much of a fight. "OK. Mine's an Erdinger. Playing it safe, I guess." Grinning at the American's somewhat conformist approach to the exploration of beers, he gestured authoritatively at the server and issued his mandate.

Cracking his knuckles loudly and elaborately, the suave Russian settled down to the task in hand. "I don't know whether it's bad form to talk shop after hours over beers, but I couldn't help but go over the discussion we had yesterday." "Oh? Which part?" asked Otto. Imbibing a long draught of his dry hopped ale, Vadim dabbed his mouth with a serviette before answering. "You recall when we were discussing the readily available supply of private wealth waiting to be poured into R&D projects, such as those which your nerdery characters are working on every day?" Otto nodded his confirmation.

"Well, it just so happens that I was chairing a meeting last night that consisted of myself and 4 ultra-high net worth individuals. Me sitting here in San Francisco, one gentleman in the Bahamas, another in the Seychelles, another in the Hamptons and the final gentleman on his yacht, somewhere off the coast of Greece, I believe. Satellite technology is so outstanding, don't you think? No, forget that. All communication technology is absolutely fantastic," gushed Vadim with a sparkle in his eyes. He had Otto's attention.

"So anyway, the main agenda of this gathering was to discuss in a private forum what type of investment opportunities these individuals were looking for and more specifically into what areas." He looked at Otto squarely. "Have you done much in the field of predictive analytics?" "Yes, of course I have. What gives?" Vadim continued. "The reason I ask is because the guy who was on the yacht in the Adriatic sea or wherever he was, asked me specifically whether I knew of any technologist, hacker or developer who had the capability to build an advanced AI prediction engine which could be taught to not only accurately foresee events, but to tell the user the best solution out of every possible scenario." Otto felt a sudden pounding in his chest.

All the noise which emanated from surrounding conversations, music and chatter seemed to be sucked out of the room as it began to blur before his very eyes. This was very likely a pivotal moment. Could this be his big opportunity? Wondering at the possibilities, he was struck by an alarming alternative. Was he about to be pipped to the post and effectively *lose his baby*? The project which had seemingly come to him via divine inspiration, a gift from god.

He wasn't materialistic and the potentially lucrative sums were not his primary motivation, but the recognition of his contribution, his being the creator of the machine, certainly was. "Are you OK, Otto?" asked Vadim with apparent concern. "I'm fine, just need a glass of water," he said, faking a cough and a splutter. Ever conscious to maintain the impression of decorum and politeness, Drozdz hurried across to the bar and procured from the bartender a glass of iced water. Gulping down the chilled water greedily, Otto collected himself.

"Sorry about that," he said, once recovered. "It struck me that I have of course worked on predictive AI before. Camarillo were commissioned by a major national supermarket chain to come up with a pricing tool that would calculate in real time, the effects of miniscule price changes across their entire product catalogue and whether these adjustments were likely to generate a rush of shoppers during sales promotions or whether they would help to get rid of expiring stock etc." Vadim nodded, impressed and getting the firm sense that things were going to plan. He had dangled a carrot and the rabbit was sniffing around it.

"I know a fair amount about it," he declared, looking across at Vadim to try and ascertain whether he was convinced of the fact. "I don't doubt it. The thing is, it's not the first time I have heard of someone trying to develop a tool which aligns quite closely with what the gentleman was asking for. Whilst I don't think that anyone has come up with the finished article yet, I do believe that it's only a matter of time until someone does...and when they do - boy, will that person be rich!" *As long as they've taken steps to secure the IP and applied for a patent*, thought Otto, witting in his keen awareness of the fact. This was becoming quite painful. If what Vadim was saying could be believed (and strangely, he didn't doubt the veracity of it) then there was a real risk that someone somewhere could get there before him. He wasn't used to failure, or not finishing first and the very fear of this eventuality almost made him feel nauseous. He couldn't let it happen and resolved that his only option was to put some skin in the game.

Looking directly into Vadim's eyes, he decided to go gung-ho and adopt a cavalier approach. It was now or never, he reasoned. An image of Charles Barker appeared in his mind's eye, presented as an untimely visual reminder of someone who he felt he could absolutely trust, but had decided not to unload his worries onto when he'd had the chance. "Incidentally, I've been working on something in my spare time which could be construed as *crossing into* the realms of what your client was looking for." He realised that he was dancing around the handbags somewhat, but felt that he had to tread carefully on this one.

Knowing full well that this disclosure would follow and enjoying the delicious inevitability of watching his opponent fall right into his trap filled Drozdz with a masochistic buzz. Feigning mild surprise, the Russian suitably adjusted his facial expression. "Oh? How so?" Otto went on to elaborate his great idea, continuing to dance around the edges at first, but steadily revealing more and more of his treasured secret. Drozdz couldn't quite believe how quickly the young engineer had taken his concept from nebulous whiteboarding to a basic operational proof of concept. He even managed to find a grudging respect for the achievement despite a deeply-rooted mistrust in his heart for what the man opposite him apparently stood for, the country of his birth, the ideology, indeed all of it.

After listening to Otto's increasingly revealing account of his considerable undertaking, Vadim leant back with a look of genuine commendation. "That," he began with great gravity, "sounds like an almost exact fit of what the gentleman asked for." The two of them temporarily sat there in silence, mulling the repercussions over. The server swept up to their table and enquired if they would care for another couple of beers. "Same again?" suggested Vadim. He nodded and the server went over to pour their drinks. "Will you excuse me for a couple of minutes," said Otto as he stood up and made his way to the restroom. Vadim inclined his head in the affirmative and watched Otto make his way across the room.

Once he has was safely out of sight, he reached covertly into his pocket and located a miniscule vial which contained a curious-looking dark liquid - a potentially lethal concoction which sat squarely at the centre of his plan to take control away from Otto that night and slip away into the night without trace. The fact that common side effects of this poison included brain damage, if not severe mental impairment, mattered not in the least to the Russian.

The two fresh beers arrived and to the delight of Drozdz, Otto was still not back from the bathroom. Glancing carefully in all directions to ensure that no-one was observing him, he made a show of raising Otto's glass into the air as if to admire the golden beverage from all angles as a connoisseur might. Keeping guard with practised concentration, he began to unscrew with his spare hand, the little ampoule.

Washing his hands and watching himself in the mirror, Otto cut an aggravated figure. He couldn't have felt any more stressed than he did at that moment. He needed time to think and digest everything that had been said. It wasn't in his nature to rush decisions, especially momentous ones such as these. He took one last determined look into the mirror and attempted to psyche himself up. Just then his phone beeped to announce a collection of incoming messages. There was one from Stella which told him that she was just leaving the office and would be heading home to shower and change before heading out to her Japanese evening class. He replied to the effect that he was about to have his 2nd beer with that Vadim character he'd mentioned and so far, it was all very interesting.

The other message was from Trang in Singapore. It caught Otto's attention immediately. *I have no recollection of that name. Are you sure he's legit?* He felt that familiar ostinato beat in his chest, a rapid and regular thumping rhythm which brought to mind that familiar cloud of confusion and uncertainty. On the one hand, everything appeared to check out - the guy's name appeared where it should when Googled; he had a LinkedIn profile, appeared on various business directories, his search firm did exist, albeit with a very cryptic holding page that gave little clue as to the activities or focus areas of that particular business.

However, he had indicated the secretive nature of what he did. He fired a quick message back to Trang. *I ran some basic searches. He appears to check out, but I've only gained a high level view. Can you look into him for me?* By requesting this favour, he knew his friend would do a solid job. There were few better hackers or more dedicated researchers out there who would happily spend hours digging where others either wouldn't think to or who had long since given up on the task. Straightening the edges of his jacket and brushing imaginary dust from his trousers, he again looked in the mirror. Fortifying himself for what might come next in the discussion, he stepped back out of the restroom.

By some merciful decree of fate, just as Drozdz had been about to slip a few poisonous drops of his black liquid into Otto's beer, the server had reappeared, much to Vadim's disgust. They began in the most earnest and apologetic of tones to provide a lengthy and detailed presentation with the aim of showcasing their wide-ranging beer selection for that month. "Hey! I'm Dwayne and I'll be your server this evening. Tonight we have a wonderful selection of beers including *California Gold* which was so called after the gold rush which began in Sierra Nevada in 1848…" Vadim almost growled out loud in his displeasure.

The server breezily went on until they caught sight of Drozdz's hostile expression, his eyes alone being enough to frighten away wild horses. Breaking off mid-sentence, the server gingerly dropped the beer menu at arm's length softly onto the edge of the table as someone might dispose of a reeking diaper. No sooner had the server ambled away, Otto reappeared. With no time to serve up a dose of his lethal medicine and cursing inwardly, Drozdz made a good enough disguise of his movements to ensure that Otto could have no suspicion. "I got you another *Erdinger*. Myself, I changed tack and went for an *Eagle Cap*." Otto thanked him and took another draught. It occurred to him that his fitness routine was somewhere suffering over these last few days and he resolved to put that right as soon as possible.

"Tell me, Otto. This machine you say you've dabbled with." "Built. I've actually built it." Vadim's eyes widened like saucers. "Get away!" Nodding knowingly, Otto derived a flush of pride from this latest reaction of Vadim. "You know, Otto. When you said that you had developed a machine that can leverage predictive technology in that way, I assumed that you simply had the framework, or at best the theory down on paper. However, if I understand you correctly, you've gone a few steps beyond that?! Geez." Vadim raised a glass as if he were saluting a triumphant comrade. "Kudos! That is simply incredible. What a feat of engineering!" Clinking glasses, Otto afforded himself a smile. "You should be proud of yourself, man," continued Vadim.

Otto looked down at the floor in an unassuming manner. "I'm not really the type to blow my own trumpet." "Sure, I agree. "Where vanity ends, reason ends too." Vadim looked broody for a moment. "Who said that," asked Otto. "I don't recall," replied Vadim. "Perhaps it was a Russian," suggested Otto helpfully. "It does have a Russian feel to it." Stroking the neck of his beer glass, Vadim nodded in contemplation.

Returning to his theme, he pursued his course. "Let's just suppose for example, you wanted to take your product to market." He scanned Otto's expression carefully before going on. "I assume you've thought about it?" "Sure, I've thought about it…but it's early days. The product isn't anywhere near ready for market yet." *So he's probably not even registered a patent or copyrighted the IP yet* mused Vadim. *This is good. This is very good.*

Now Vadim played to the ego and tailored his blue sky pitch in the way he knew it would best appeal to Otto. "You can just imagine the recognition that this person will get. The accolades for developing something so advanced. It could almost be the defining technological breakthrough of our age. Imagine the girls throwing themselves at you. Imagine the fast cars, private jets, tropical island mansion, champagne on top."

As Drozdz delivered this picture of the unrestrained, avaricious American dream, he felt a deep sense of disgust in his own mind at the mere fact that he was promoting it as though it were a good thing or something to be aspired to; indeed his parents would have spun in their graves if they could have heard him. He quelled his internal discomfort by reminding himself that this was purely a means to an end. It was simply the case that he had to do what was required to achieve his objectives and complete his mission.

Otto for his part, didn't feel any particular excitement about the trappings of such a lifestyle, but as Vadim had correctly ascertained, he was driven by recognition for his achievements and the longer the Russian went on, the more he was drawn into the spider's web.

After the 3rd beer had gone down, Otto's resistance had been eroded to the point where his guard had lowered dangerously and his judgement was beginning to be impacted. "It's unfortunate that I have to fly back to Boston tomorrow. It would have been good to see this machine in action," probed Vadim. Otto, in possession of his normal inhibitions, would never have even considered offering a demo to someone who was to all intents and purposes, an outsider, but with a loose tongue and lowered guard, he foolishly gave his support for the proposal.

"You're welcome to come and take a look at it. I have a working beta on my laptop at home." Vadim glanced at his watch and made a show of being a little short on time. He had a red eye flight to Boston tomorrow, he told Otto. He didn't wish to encroach on his private life etc. Playing the psychological game like a seasoned expert, he finally submitted to the young American's enthusiasm and agreed to come over and take a look at the machine over coffee, Otto knowing little of the extreme danger he would shortly find himself in. Drozdz by now, a firm friend in Otto's eyes, deserved an Oscar for the animalistic intelligence with which he played his role. It was akin to the fox circling the chicken coop, slowly by degrees gaining trust before moving in for the kill. Poor Otto was hopelessly exposed and in over his head. He just didn't know it yet.

Chapter 15

The taxi driver on the way back to Otto's apartment turned out to be of Polish origin and upon discovering this, Drozdz and he entered into a lively and spirited conversation in that flowing Slavic tongue, not a word of which Otto was able to follow and so he passed the 10 minute journey in relative peace. It was 8.38pm and so he figured there was time to make coffee, give Vadim a high-level overview of the platform and send him on his way before Stella was due at 9.30pm.

It wasn't like he was being rude or anything - he knew that Vadim had an early flight to catch out of SFO, so in his mind he would be doing him a favour. He just didn't want him to fly out of there without first being sold on the machine. There was a risk, Otto felt, that someone else might jump in there ahead of time and steal his opportunity away. In his mind, this was a chance that he didn't want to let slip. Normally he wouldn't have invited a stranger into his home, but for the bigger picture, it was a risk he was willing to take.

They arrived just before a quarter to nine Otto's apartment building. Darkness had fallen and the street was unusually deserted. It seemed that there was nobody about as they climbed the steps out front. "Coffee?" offered Otto. "Thank you, that'd be great." "Please, take a seat," instructed Otto, sweeping his hand toward the sofa. "I'll be right with you." He then strolled off to the kitchen to make the arrangements. Vadim looked all around the room, scrutinising as he'd been trained from a young age, to take in every detail, flesh out a mental map of the building's blueprint and above all, to know your escape route if it became necessary to flee.

Whilst waiting for the coffee to brew, Otto's phone started ringing. It was a video call from Trang. He made a quick mental calculation. It would have been coming up to 1pm in Singapore. Sliding his finger across, he answered the call. His friend appeared on the screen in an unusually ruffled looking state. He had worry all over his face and unusually for him, he bypassed the usual jokey pleasantries and went straight to the point. "Where are you right now?" he demanded. "I'm at home, why?" "OK, I need you to listen to me," he said breathlessly. Instantly, he had grabbed Otto's attention.

"That Vadim Drozdz guy doesn't exist. I dug a little deeper and it's a fake profile. I ran searches on FBI databases, Interpol, you name it - he's not a real person." Trang delivered this urgent message with agitation as though he were conscious of something Otto wasn't. "You need to call the cops. I don't think this guy wants to be friends with you for the sake of your good looks." This vague attempt at humour which was delivered in such a serious tone of voice that it only served to unsettle him and did nothing to relieve the renewed confusion he was feeling. "Our video calls have all been hacked by someone on the dark web!" Suddenly a commanding voice directly behind Otto startled him. "Cut that call."

He spun around in shock only to collide directly into Drozdz who had treaded softly into the kitchen unawares. "Now!" bellowed the imposing Russian. Trang, becoming visibly animated, began to shout wildly on the other end of the line but Drozdz snatched the phone out of Otto's hands and in a shocking and sudden display of violence, flung it with all his might at the floor where it shattered into pieces. Otto stood, rooted to the spot, shaking, stunned and simply unable to comprehend what had just happened.

His heart was beating uncontrollably, and he wondered whether this was what it was like when you were about to be seized by a heart attack. Those piercing, pale blue eyes were fixed upon him again, laser-like in their mesmerising effect. Vadim spoke in a new and menacing tone which Otto had not heard before. All of that prior friendliness had evaporated without warning into thin air and he realised now with rapidly growing awareness that he was in serious trouble.

"Let me guess. Trang Nguyen, right? Our mutual friend." He said the name with such narcissism that Otto was overcome by a wave of nausea. Feeling increasingly unsteady on his feet, he wobbled as a spate of dizziness struck him and reached out for the corner of the worktop in order to locate something, anything to which he could anchor himself. Drozdz misreading the action as an intention on Otto's part to reach for an object which might be used as a weapon, shot out a meaty arm in the blink of an eye and grabbed the American by the wrist.

His vice-like grip sent pain shooting up Otto's arm and he refrained immediately from seeking stability and pawed at Drozdz's arm in a bid to be released from the agonising hold. "You are going to do something for me, Mr Delvecchio. I need hardly warn you not to disobey my requests. I *will* cause you a great deal of pain. Possibly worse. I haven't decided yet. Do we understand each other?" His every fibre throbbed with naked fear. The sheer terror that coursed through his veins was like nothing else he had ever experienced in his life. "Yes," he almost whispered to his captor. "What?!" yelled Drozdz at the top of his voice. "I can't hear you, Otto. You're going to have to speak up!"

Roaring these instructions directly into the subjugated ear of Otto, as bullies tend to, he was getting a real kick out of terrorising his victim. "Get up," snarled Drozdz, forcibly hauling Otto like a rag doll to his feet. Frogmarching the American through his own apartment and back into the living room where his laptop sat closed on the sofa, he threw him with some force toward that item of furniture. Otto, glad at least of a soft landing, unfurled like a tattered flag on the sofa, before hurriedly scrambling to sit back up.

Adopting an authoritative pose with hands on hips, Drozdz made clear his objectives. "First, you are going to give me a high level overview of what you have built. Then you are going to extract the entire machine, complete with source code into a zip file which you will transfer directly into this 2 terabyte flash drive." At this, he held up what looked like a solid gold USB drive, no larger than a matchbox and almost certainly a product which wasn't available to the general public.

Having little choice in the matter, Otto did as he was instructed and proceeded to log into the laptop. A secretive glance at the clock told him that it was 9.08pm. He realised with a sinking feeling that Stella was due to arrive in the next 20 to 30 minutes. She would be completely unaware that he had a visitor and felt his blood running cold when he considered the risks she faced in coming into his home that night. He wondered if there was any possibility of getting a message to her, of sending a warning somehow. It didn't seem possible. He watched as his prized project loaded up on the screen before him. The project which had consumed so much of his spare time and consumed so much of his thought process.

A true magnum opus of which he was now facing the very real possibility of having stolen from him. Drozdz prodded him sharply. "Get on with it!" There was no chance but to comply with the edict. Fingers shaking uncontrollably, he forced himself to gain a semblance of control over them. Multiple thoughts, all of them fragmented and disparate zoomed through his head as he grappled furiously to rein in his rising panic. The password box appeared on screen. With bitter regret, he guided the mouse and clicked the cursor inside the box where it flashed slowly, like a distress signal. If he could have programmed it to send out his own personal SOS, he would have done. That was wishful thinking however, with an angry ogre standing over him, watching his every move like a bird of prey.

A strange feeling came over Otto unexpectedly; he looked up at his captor. "What exactly are you planning to do with my software?" Before he knew what had happened, a searing pain flooded through his head, causing him to adopt the brace position and cower between the table and sofa. Drozdz had struck him on the ear with considerable force, completely out of the blue and for no apparent reason other than sadistic pleasure. Standing over the disorientated programmer, the towering frame of the brute loomed large, casting an ominous shadow on the nearby wall.

"Let me help you out, Mr Delvecchio. I will be asking the questions around here." He was relishing every second of his tyrannical domination. "Secondly, it is well known that a programmer requires his or her hands to perform their basic function." The unfortunate Otto didn't understand at first where Drozdz was going with this, but feared the worst based on the way events were unfolding. "You need your fingers! Otherwise, how will you write code?" He pointed directly at Otto as the other looked up at him helplessly, like a bloodied rabbit in a trap. Drozdz let out a maniacal laugh. It was the kind of laugh only a truly deranged psychopath might exhibit.

Otto would have done anything to escape the situation he found himself in. As far as basic needs went, he would have been grateful for a simple glass of water, but didn't dare broach the subject with this vindictive monster. It was clear that basic human rights counted for nothing in this man's eyes - that much was obvious. He imagined what time it must be. 9.15pm? He was apprehensive beyond words about the impending visit of his new girlfriend. Surely, she was now also in danger and would fall directly into the same trap as Otto. He had no way of warning her off or telling her to seek help. Drozdz turned on his heel abruptly and took a few steps, reaching for his jacket which was hung on the hat stand in the entrance hall. Otto remained cowering where he was, too frightened to move until instructed.

When he saw what Drozdz had retrieved from his inside pocket, he froze stone dead. It was a penknife. Walking with slow deliberation back toward him so that he might crank up the terror a further notch or two, the oppressor slowly folded out a blade. Turning it over, this way and that, examining it before folding it back in and taking out the next blade, he went on in this way for at least a couple of minutes, knowing and taking great enjoyment from the fact that Otto was watching him in abject dread. "Hah!" exclaimed Drozdz with a bear-like roar and stamped his foot loudly on the wooden floor. "This one will be perfect." In a split second, he lunged across the room and seized the little finger of Otto's left hand.

Unable to stop himself from shouting out, the distressed victim screamed out the word "No!" Drozdz brandished a sardonic grin, a truly terrifying look in his eyes. "Ah. Have you remembered the password?" His question was laced with cruelty and a knowledge that he held total and utter control over the young American. Otto nodded vigorously, trying to ignore the palpitations he felt in his chest. Drozdz simply pointed at the computer screen, indicating for Otto to continue.

In went the password and so for the first time, the user interface of his brainchild was revealed to an outsider. Drozdz watched intently as Otto fired up the query machine in readiness for whatever the invader wanted to ask of it. Just as he was doing so, within the framework of the lines of code, something out of the corner of his eye caught his attention. Trying to avoid focusing his gaze on it for more than a second at a time lest his Russian captor notice and follow his eyeline, he felt a surge of excitement well up from the pit of his stomach. It was a hidden message, embedded within the lines of code.

Only one other person in his network knew how to write in this code, let alone think to try such an audacious stunt. This message could only have been sent by Trang. He could have cried with the sense of relief he felt at knowing that someone might be aware of what was going on and consequently be in a position to seek help. He glanced furtively at the Russian, but his gaze was firmly trained on the screen and it didn't so far appear - touch wood - that he had picked up on the secret implanted message which, in order to be seen, one had to quite literally "read between the lines." Maintaining the hugely stressful balancing act of translating the hidden message one second at a time whilst his eyes were required to keeping flicking around the entire screen, all whilst trying simultaneously to buy time before he was asked to input a query, he deduced as quickly as he could what Trang had encoded into the intricate tapestry of the platform's architecture.

Message left with EA of your CTO. VD = agent of corporate espionage. Police notified but not classified as serious. Sending for help. Stand by.

A cocktail of mixed emotions washed over Otto. *How the hell could this not be classed as serious?* he thought to himself, angrily. At the same time, he felt relief and heartfelt thanks for his friend's ingenuity but he was acutely aware that not only was he running out of time with which to stall his detainer, Stella was likely to arrive at any moment.

As if things couldn't get any worse, the buzzer sounded and the voice of Stella, normally so welcome to him, announced her arrival through the hallway speaker.

Chapter 16

Drozdz took a firm hold of Otto's neck. "Who's the girl?" he demanded, irate at this unexpected event for which he'd not been given sufficient time to create a contingency plan. "A colleague of mine from work," came the weak reply. Drozdz was clearly trying to come up with a plan on the hoof. "OK. Here's what's going to happen. You tell her that you just woke up and that you're not feeling great." He continued to think on his feet. So far, this wasn't the worst of demands in the sense that it might give him a premise to send her away. Even better, knowing as she did that they had both agreed for her to come around after her evening class, she might hopefully get the sense that something was wrong and to go and raise the alarm. Then again, he wondered, wouldn't Vadim surely think of this eventuality?

"Wait," announced Drozdz. On 2nd thoughts, invite her in. She can keep us company." The now familiar surge of dread flooded through Otto's whole being and his heart sank at the realisation that if Stella walked straight into the trap, not only was she in danger but their hopes of raising the alarm were dashed. He was left only to rely on whatever help Trang had asked for, but even then, if the police weren't willing to even investigate his concerns, was there any realistic escape for them both? There was no knowing what this nasty piece of work would do in order to get what he came for and so exposing Stella to the clear and present danger that existed was that last thing he wished to do.

The buzzer sounded again. *Maybe she would walk away*, Otto considered. *Yes, please God.* By the same token, he should have considered what she would likely be thinking. She might imagine that he'd got so drunk he'd passed out, or taken another girl home. He felt certain that the last thing on her mind would be that some homicidal maniac had wormed his way into his confidence and kidnapped him in his own home whilst trying to steal a world-changing AI technology.

"Let's take a walk," ordered Drozdz, dragging Otto along the room toward the buzzer. "If you try to play any games with me, I swear to you that I will take off the first fingertip right now." A thin film of sweat began to build on Otto's brow. The pressure he was under was intolerable. He had to find a way out of this dire situation. He pressed the intercom and spoke into the microphone. "Hey, honey." It wasn't easy to try and hide his disquiet, but he had to do it if he hoped to retain possession of his digits.

"What took you so long?" she asked, with an ever so slight trace of irritation. "I fell asleep on the couch," he replied. There was incredulous silence. Terrified of receiving a sudden blow to the head or worse, Otto played it as safely as he possibly could, but it was like walking a tightrope between two skyscrapers with a sheer drop below. There was no room for error and he remained stuck in a highly compromised situation.

"Well, aren't you going to invite me in?" Otto's eyes darted upwards to meet with Vadim's. He nodded gravely. "You betcha." Pressing the button to grant her access, he felt his grip on the situation, indeed his sanity in general loosening, like an unravelling ball of yarn. If he'd had a gun to his head at that very moment, he couldn't have felt any more powerless. What he didn't realise and which might have served to provide some grounds for optimism is that a few strides away, in the living room, his clever and resourceful friend Trang had managed to set up a live video feed using the webcam built into Otto's laptop without any trace nor indication of having done so, with the net result of the last 30 minutes being fully recorded, documented and live streamed directly to a private server farm based in Jurong Bay, Singapore.

He had even shared an open access link with the FBI's cybersecurity division, sent from an anonymous source and completely untraceable of course. Not only was he providing full, uncensored and indisputable evidence of Drozdz's actions since the laptop was opened, thus incriminating the Russian spy in the process, he was safeguarding his friend's great invention from external piracy. However, Otto had no way of knowing this and remained rooted in his present malaise with his new girlfriend unknowingly about to enter the fray.

Drozdz flicked out a blade from his penknife which shined menacingly under the spotlights.

He looked at Otto with an expression that expressly forbade any diversion from compliance, making a throat cutting gesture for good measure. He backed into the nearest doorway and wiggled his finger toward him, indicating that Otto should move toward him. Ensuring that his prisoner remained comfortably within striking distance should he decide to make a break for freedom, or to warn the colleague, he backed into the doorframe out of sight from the entrance. An agonising wait ensued as Stella made her way from the street up to Otto's floor. At length, she arrived and presented herself at his front door.

She stopped short of the doorframe and gaped wide-eyed at him. "What the heck happened to you? You look like you've gone 5 rounds with Mike Tyson," she exclaimed with unfeigned horror. Improvising on the spot, trying desperately to avoid provoking the beast that was hidden in the shadows, he offered another feeble excuse. "I feel like I have!" She hesitated before crossing the threshold. He rather wished she had stayed where she was, but it was inevitable that she would enter his apartment and sure enough, she resumed her forward movement after a short pause.

Struggling against the odds to hold his agitation in check, she walked right up to him and stopped just a matter of inches from his face. Where she would normally have sought a kiss, this time she stopped, emitting a jumble of feminal signals. There was maternal instinct. There was suspicion. There was concern. All of these intense feelings emitted through a kind of invisible radar system to Otto.

He needed only to look at her face to understand in an instant what was passing through Stella's mind and what she was thinking. It was almost telepathic in its transmission. The mutual understanding didn't last long, being rudely snatched away from them with another burst of savagery from the Russian spy who lurked in the shadows. Stella yelped aloud in shock at the unanticipated discordance which shattered their former tranquillity; Drozdz leaping powerfully out of his dark corner, completely ambushed the both of them and knocked them to the floor before they knew what was happening.

The element of surprise being a long-advantageous component of many a battle strategy throughout history, Drozdz was a past master in such tactics. He was always a couple of steps ahead and operated adroitly with the nimble skills of a master strategist. Speaking both commandingly and decisively, he issued his instructions. "Right! Both of you. Into the living room. Now!" Otto, being more conscious of the ever-present danger and by this point fully cognizant of the lengths to which Drozdz would go, complied immediately whereas Stella who hadn't had the benefit of hindsight was very much fresh blood in this gruesome, nerve wracking scenario.

Struggling to her feet, she was positively simmering with rage, seething with the outrage of it all. "Who the f**k do you think you are? Do you know who you're f**king with?" Her protestations were ruthlessly cut short with a blow to the temple, upon receipt of which, she fell silent and dropped like a stone to the floor, motionless. Otto, seeing this remorseless action, cried out and charged at the midriff of Drozdz. Knowing what was coming a mile off, the big Russian adeptly swerved to the left as Otto, coming toward him at speed and by now fully committed, carried on forward with uncontrollable momentum and went crashing straight into a hefty wooden dresser.

Before he was even allowed his inevitable collapse onto the floor, Drozdz weighed in with a powerful blow to the kidneys, adding a side order of bruising to Otto's already maimed anatomy. Satisfying himself that his victim wasn't going anywhere, he turned his attention to the American woman. Clumping across the wooden floorboards, he seized the pretty girl by the hair, to the point where she shrieked in pain.

"So you're his colleague are you? Maybe you mean more to him? Let's see." With that, he let go of her hair and gave her a great shove, sending her spinning toward the sofa. He was a true barbarian, of that there was no doubt. Back in Moscow, he was described as 'Yudashkin's protege' and it was not difficult to see why. The mindset, the steadfast sense of loyalty to Mother Russia, the archetypal hatred of the West - it was all there in his makeup. At that point he seemed to dismiss Stella as nothing more than a weak American of no consequence. She was worth nothing to him and had nothing of value to contribute.

Better to let her remain splayed on the sofa and watch the rest of the show. Retrieving his knife from his jacket pocket, he folded out the sharpest of all 8 blades. "Now...," he announced, walking across the room to Otto and clutching in his grasp, the programmer's right hand. "Eeny, meeny, miny, mo. Which finger stays, which finger goes?" he chanted under his breath as a kind of sick mantra. From her incapacitated position on the sofa, Stella pleaded with him, but he simply mocked her by repeating the heartfelt sentiments she expressed right back at her in a high pitched, artificial American accent. It looked to be game over for Otto as the malignant bully started to make a sawing motion with his blade in the air and slowly, deliberately lowered the blade down toward his victim's little finger. It came down to a matter of choice, Otto reasoned. Either to die fighting or to submit without a struggle. He chose the former. Just prior to the blade making contact with his little finger, he summoned all the remaining strength he could muster by aiming a sharp kick with his extended leg directly at the groin of Drozdz.

It came as a totally unexpected shock to the pernicious Russian. He howled in agony and dropped to the floor like a topple statue, clutching his wounded genitals. Stella, sensing this incredible opportunity sprang into action like a brave lion, grabbing the nearest weapon, which was in this case, Otto's laptop. Taking an almighty swing, she skipped across the room with the sprightly agility of a tomcat and made significant contact with the head of Drozdz before he knew what had hit him. Ignoring the stinging pain which tore through his body like an electric current, Otto leapt into action in support of his brave girlfriend and put Drozdz into a decisive headlock, putting all of his power into choking his oppressor into submission. He knew that he wasn't the strongest guy in the world, but he knew the law of averages and felt that by holding an opponent in a sufficiently tight headlock, there was only the smallest chance that he might break out of it, particularly if he kept the rest of his body out of reach. He had watched his younger brother attend a series of Judo championships whilst growing up and had learnt that much from his sibling. Little did he know that it would one day save his life.

The clear and obvious mistake that Drozdz had made was in becoming too confident and believing that he had full control over them both. Once he had decided that he would proceed with cutting Otto's fingertips off, he assumed that his opponent had given up and thrown the towel in. As a result, he was wrong and by making such an assumption, he left the smallest of windows available, which Otto subsequently took full advantage of by disabling him with a decisive blow to the most vulnerable part of his body. The fact that Stella in her bravery was sufficiently well positioned to take advantage of and reinforce their position was simply the icing on the cake.

Drozdz struggled like a caged beast, writhing and thrashing furiously. Given his considerable advantages in strength, it was touch and go as to whether Otto would be able to hold him off, so Stella applied a further, resounding crack to his groin with the laptop which went some way to subduing their torturer. Regardless of the cost of replacing his laptop - should that have become a necessity - it wasn't something he cared about just then. Everything he had worked on was backed up in the cloud, so he could relax on that score - there would be no danger of losing the fruits of his labour. As if by magic, there was an urgent rapping on the door. A clamour of voices bellowed that it was the San Francisco police department. Keen to avoid any further damage which might well have resulted as a consequence of having his door smashed open with a battering ram, Otto requested with some urgency that Stella go and let them in. Happily complying with his request, she did so and accompanied by an assortment of officers in full riot gear was none other than Charles Barker. His first sight of Otto was of his star player sitting squarely on top of the bad guy, holding him steadfastly in a headlock. He couldn't resist a whimsical joke. "Jesus, Otto. I'm not paying you to beat the shit out of the competition as well!"

After all the mess and confusion had been cleared up, it became clear that the man masquerading as Vadim Drozdz was actually of unknown origin and identity. All they knew was that he was in all likelihood a Russian operative who was on some kind of corporate espionage mission to wrestle classified company information from Otto. He knew now that he would have to reveal the details of his secret project to Charles Barker before he got in any deeper. After explaining the genesis of his idea through to completion, his CTO simply looked at him and gave a rueful smile. "Otto, I'm so glad you told me in the end. I appreciate that by working on this thing in the evenings, you didn't actually break any rules, but geez. You could've come to me with this. What were you thinking?" A little tut of disapproval followed and Otto reddened. There wasn't much he could say. He knew he had gone down a rabbit hole and could have ended up seriously maimed, or worse killed.

The murderous look in Drozdz's eyes as he was escorted out of the apartment by three bulky riot police was a chilling enough spectacle for anyone and Otto felt a massive sense of relief at his removal, no doubt as did Stella. Discussions around convalescence were held and it was decided at the recommendation of Charles Barker that Otto should be given 6 months' leave of absence.

Barker ultimately acted as a go-between in negotiations with the senior management team on how they should best utilise Otto's innovation whilst ensuring that his overwhelming contribution was rightly recognised. Superfluous items such as route-to-market, pricing, terms of licensing and so forth held little interest for the creator. He just wanted his contribution to be known, recognised and appreciated. It was clear to him that Charles Barker had his back and held no grudge on account of Otto holding back on his after-hours project. In the end, preparations were made to run the platform through beta testing, the marketing department was summoned and given the brief directly by the CEO to ready a comprehensive and wide ranging campaign to drive awareness and encourage early subscriptions. The potential risk of misuse was strongly emphasised via Barker to the board and a compromise was reached whereby the licensing agreements in all territories were wrapped up tight and carefully crafted legal language which in turn allowed little wriggle room for usage outside any law-abiding, moral or ethical purposes.

The removal and subsequent prosecution of Drozdz ultimately changed nothing politically; ostensibly he was utilised by the untouchables in power as a simple patsy i.e. someone who is easily blamed or made a scapegoat to pay the metaphorical bill for a political fallout, as was apparently the case with Lee Harvey Oswald in the assassination of John F Kennedy in 1963. Whilst Drozdz was detained and tried by the Americans, under the American justice system in an American court, political expediency and protectionism put paid to any hope of his bosses or superiors themselves being exposed and brought to justice. Ultimately, protectionism and closed ranks ensured that the truth of the matter which, if anyone had cared or been brave enough to investigate it, would have taken its surveyor along a long and winding road that eventually led to the upper echelons of the Kremlin.

The happy couple looked out of the aeroplane window. The landmass below looked alien, yet curiously inviting. Certainly in Otto's case, as a first time visitor, it all looked exceptionally exciting. The country positively begged to be explored. A whole month of sightseeing lay ahead of them. Hot air springs, sushi, cherry blossom, ramen, robot restaurants, bamboo forests, Shinto shrines, bullet trains, Mount Fuji, sumo and sake. He was so excited. Taking his hand in hers, she rolled her thumb lovingly over the surface of his knuckles. "I've always wanted to visit Japan," he said with boyish enthusiasm. "Well, today you will," she replied, lovingly.